RETURNING PRIDE

THE PRIDE SERIES

JILL SANDERS

GRAYTON

To my brothers & sisters
without whom,
I would have been a
very lonely child.

SUMMARY

*E*verything seems to be going Iian's way, he has a successful restaurant, a beautiful home, family, and friends. He's even overcome the loss of his hearing, but why does he still feel like something is missing.

Allison has worked hard to make a name for herself in the art world, now all she wants is peace and quiet to work on her passion. But, with her mother overtaken by illness, she has less time than ever. When everything is stripped away in one tragic blow, and she's being stalked by a madman, she'll need the help of her hometown and an old flame, to turn everything around and find what she's been looking for.

CHAPTER 1

*O*verlooking the water, Iian watched as the waves crashed violently on the rocks below the cliffs. Winter was almost over, yet the cold seemed to hang in the air. Low dark clouds hovered over the dark horizon as mist clung all around him. The rain had stopped an hour earlier, leaving a lingering scent in the breeze that hit his face. This was his home; he belonged here and just knew it. He could see the lights from fishing boats, they were scattered along the shoreline. Though unable to hear, he knew fog horns would be sounding, signaling their warning of the jagged shore.

It had been over ten years since his accident, which had left him without his father, and without his hearing. The nightmares of that day still haunted him. He couldn't remember all the details, but his memories played like a broken record in his head.

It took him almost a year to get over his physical wounds. Learning a new language had been hard for him, even harder on his brother and sister, Todd and Lacey. Sign language was now something he did without thinking. The pain of losing their father, however, had taken a lot longer for them to get over.

Their father had been the glue that had held their family together, after the loss of their mother at Iian's birth. His father had worked hard at the restaurant that had been his parents' dream, making enough to start his own business, Jordan Shipping, which Iian's brother Todd now ran. After their father's death, his sister Lacey had stepped in and taken over the role of holding everyone together.

After losing his hearing, Iian started noticing a few things happening to him. He noticed his eyesight, his sense of smell, and his taste had sharpened immensely. These enhancements had helped with his career as a chef but lowered his ability to deal with other people.

He knew what everyone saw in him. He was tall, standing a little over six-and-a-half feet. He had been rail thin until about the ninth grade when he'd hit his last growth spurt. He worked out regularly and since his youth had added to his bulk with lean muscles, which he was proud of. His dark hair and light crystal eyes were a family trait, as well as the small cleft in his chin.

As he pushed his hair out of his eyes, he stood on the small cliff and looked around. To his left, columns of smoke rose from houses in the small tight-knit community of Pride, Oregon. He could just make out the green roof of The Golden Oar, his restaurant, his life. The larger, old building sat on the waterfront, just off the main street in town. The place had been his sole focus since his accident. He'd been raised working in the kitchen or the dining halls, it had been in his blood. Handed down from several generations, now the place was his, coming to him on his twenty-fifth birth-day. It was a good thing that cooking was in his blood, it just happened to be a bonus that it was his passion as well.

He could think of only one other thing he'd felt this way about, and he was wondering when she'd come back into town.

Allison was home, there was no doubt about it. She'd missed the old place; it had never looked so inviting. The house was dark except for the tall lamps on either side of the cement path that led to the bright blue front door. The cool evening rain was washing the sidewalk and streets, making them shine and look new.

She remembered when her father was alive, the house had been in pristine shape. Shortly after his death, money was short and they had a harder time taking care of every-thing. Well, the house had been the last thing on their minds then.

The blue shutters on the windows still hung strong, they just needed some paint. Actually, the whole house could use a fresh coat, for that matter. The inside had always been kept in tip-top shape. Her mother had always been somewhat of a perfectionist, especially when it came to her house.

Thinking of her mother, she turned off her car and real-ized that she'd always had more of a partnership rather than a mother-daughter relationship. Especially after her sister, Abby, had died.

Taking a deep breath, she opened her car door and

made a run for the front door through the pouring rain, her keys and overnight bag on-hand.

She had expected her mother to be asleep at this late hour; she'd left Los Angeles a little later than planned due to traffic, which had slowed her trip by a good two hours.

When she opened the front door, she had to jerk it open. She turned on the lights and what she found scared her. One of the couch cushions was on the floor; there was a large pile of dirty clothes in the corner by the television set, which was still on. There were dishes sitting on the coffee table that looked like they'd been there for weeks. Turning on lights, she ran into the back and was even more shocked by what she saw the kitchen. Something was definitely not right! Things were thrown around in there as well. Rushing to the back of the small house, she knocked on her mother's door as she pushed it open.

"Mom? Can I come in? Mom is everything okay?" She shoved the door, pushing clothes that had piled up behind it.

Allison saw a small lump in the bed and quickly switched on the light. Her mother's face was pale and thin. She must have lost at least ten pounds since she'd seen her around six months ago. Her curly, black hair was streaked with silver and stuck straight up, giving her an *"I've just seen a ghost,"* look. It was her mother's eyes that worried her the most. They were red-rimmed and staring blankly and looked completely empty as her mother looked at her. Teresa Adams was in her mid-sixties and had been alone for almost a third of her life.

"Abby. Oh, your back! Did you forget your umbrella?" She attempted to sit up in bed.

"No Mama, it's me, Allison," Allison sat next to her

mother and felt her forehead, checking for a fever. Her mother's head was hot and she could see her was shaking with a fever.

"Oh, I'm sorry dear. Mommy was just taking a quick nap and you know how your father gets when you forget your umbrella. Better run and get it or you'll be late for school." Teresa started to lie back down.

"Oh, Mom," Allison leaned over. Picking up the phone, she dialed the local doctor's number from memory.

"Hello?" The voice sounded younger than the eighty-year-old man who was the normal doctor in town.

"I... I'm sorry, I think I have the wrong number," she started to hang up.

"This is Dr. Stevens. Are you looking for a doctor?"

"Yes, this is Allison Adams. My mother is running a high fever and she isn't coherent. Can you come quickly?"

"Yes, Miss Adams, I can be there in about ten minutes."

"Thank you," Allison hung up and went into the adjoining bath to get a cold cloth for her mother.

Aaron watched as his wife, Lacey, rolled over and asked, "Mrs. Adams? Is something wrong?"

"She's running a fever, her daughter called. It shouldn't take me long to deal with this. Go back to bed." He looked over at his wife, as he pulled on a pair of worn jeans and a warm sweater.

It had been three years since he'd taken over his grandfather's medical practice in Pride. Two years after his marriage to the woman who now carried their first child. He smiled down at her small form in the bed.

"Allison called? I didn't know she was back in town," Lacey said slowly sitting up. "I should go with you, see if there's something I can do," she started to rise.

"Oh, no you don't," he rushed over to place his hands on her shoulders. "If you start going on all my house calls, who's going to stay home and take care of our children?" He smiled down at her glowing face and gently laid a hand on her small but growing belly. "Besides, it's wet and cold out there. You should keep my side of the bed warm for when I come back." He leaned over and kissed her. "I should be back soon."

He was gone before she could say another word. When exactly had she lost control? Oh yeah, the day she'd bumped into him. She smiled into the pillow and remembered that wonderful hot day and quickly fell back asleep.

Allison had turned on every light while she waited for the doctor. She had just started to clean the front room when there was a quick knock on the door. She rushed over and opened the door quickly for the doctor.

"Thank God. She's just back--" she dropped off as a very tall, very wet male started to step into the light.

Taking a large step back she grabbed the only thing handy, one of her mother's favorite crystal candlesticks.

"Who are you?" She demanded holding the candlestick like a batter ready to hit a home run.

"Allison, it's me, Aaron Stevens, remember we met before," he stepped into the doorway farther, the light finally hit his face. "You were expecting my grandfather, remember, he retired," he smiled down at her. "I'd hate to go back to my wife and explain why I have stitches in my head," he said holding out his hands.

Then she remembered that he'd married Lacey. She'd even attended their wedding when they'd been married on the beach a few years back. It must be that she was tired from the long trip and maybe the worry of her mother was warping her brain. Quickly setting down her weapon, she wiped her sweaty hands on her jeans.

"Oh my god! I'm so sorry, it slipped my mind. I just drove several hours and my brain isn't in gear. Come in, my mother's in the back." She pointed him towards the back and started walking to her mother's room.

He followed her, walking past the messy front room. She noticed that he took a quick look around.

"I just got home tonight. It appears she's been sick for a while." She waved a hand at the disarray.

When they reached her mother's bedroom, Aaron got to work.

"Are you just visiting from California?" he asked while checking her mother's blood pressure.

"Yes! No! I was planning on staying, I don't know yet. I just decided to come back last week; something just called me home." How could she explain that she'd felt drawn home? That she'd felt like she'd been starved in the city. "Is she going to be okay?" She asked she knew she had a worried look on her face as she was nervously fidgeting with her hands.

"Well, to be honest, I don't like your mother's blood pressure, and her temperature really worries me. I'd like to run some more tests." He set his stethoscope down and leaned over to check the dilation of her pupils. Leaning back up he looked at her.

"Allison, I'd like to move your mother to the hospital in Edgeview. I can have an ambulance come to pick her up," He said, as her mother started to mumble and toss about.

"Yes, of course," she said, focusing on her mother's face.

"I'll just step out and make the call." Aaron walked into the living room.

Less than an hour later, when the paramedics wheeled her mother into the emergency room, Allison and Aaron was right on their heels. She saw Lacey waiting just inside the front door of the hospital. She rushed over and gave her friend a big hug, bumping lightly into her small, pregnant belly.

"It's so good to have you back," Lacey smiled at Allison. "How is she?" she asked as she turned to her husband.

"I'm going to go find out. I'll be back shortly." He gave Lacey's hand a squeeze and disappeared down the hall where they had wheeled Allison's mom.

The two women walked up to the front nurse's desk and signed in. Lacey talked to the nurse briefly, then they turned to go sit in the waiting area, which was almost empty. The two television sets were set to the same news channel, and there was an older couple sitting across the way watching the weather.

Edgeview Medical Center was the only facility within fifty miles, so naturally, sometimes it was quite full. During the short trip there, Dr. Stevens, Aaron, he'd wanted her to call him, told her he had taken over his grandfather's local office in Pride. But he confirmed that it was more for appointments and not emergencies such as this. Here, they could run blood work, do x-rays, even surgery if needed. Her mind numbed at that thought.

Lacey had stopped at the vending machines and grabbed a bottled water for each of them. "Come and sit down. Aaron will take care of your mother," she said, taking a quick sip of her water. "I didn't know you were back in town."

"I… I just got in about an hour ago. The place was messy, you know how my mom is about everything being tidy." Lacey shook her head, "I don't even know how long she'd been sick? If I hadn't gotten home tonight…"

Lacey took a good look at her, and Allison knew what she was seeing. She was a lot thinner than the last time Lacey had seen her. Her eyes felt dull and Ally felt like she needed a good night's sleep.

"You must be tired after the long drive. Why don't you try to stretch out on the couch?" Lacey patted the cushions next to her. How could she refuse? Lacey had babysat Allison and Abby a lot when they were younger. She'd been like a really cool older sister to the pair.

Resting her head back on the small couch, she realized that she was very tired, but didn't think she could fall asleep. Her mind kept going back to what she had seen at the house, how her mother had looked lost.

Even with the hum of the television, the bright lights, and the worry on her mind, she still drifted off. A few hours later, she was awakened by Dr. Stevens, who informed her they had moved her mother into a private room on the second floor. She was stable, but her fever was still holding. He told her they were running several tests and wouldn't know the results until morning.

When Allison was finally allowed to see her mother half an hour later, she walked into the room with Lacey trailing behind her. Allison was grateful for the support of her friend.

She sat in the chair closest to her mother. Aaron pulled his wife aside and had a quiet conversation with her, after which she announced that she was heading home and would be back first thing in the morning.

Then he stood next to the bed and checking the IV tubes.

"What can you tell me?"

"Not much more tonight. I'm waiting for the lab results. It shouldn't be much longer." He looked at his watch, "I'll just go check on them."

He turned and left Alison in a room with the bright lights, loud machines, and her mother laying there, drugged and sleeping.

CHAPTER 2

*I*ian knew she was back in town. He probably knew it before anyone else did. He'd sensed something was coming all day yesterday. It was hard to explain to anyone; since he'd lost his hearing, he could just feel things. At least when it came to Allison Adams.

He liked to think he was a patient man. He had, after all, learned a new way of living at the age of eighteen, and a completely new lifestyle. In all his twenty-eight-years, he'd never waited for anything as long as he'd waited for Allison Adams.

Allison had been there in first grade, her long blonde hair swinging with every step she'd made walking down the long school hallways. He remembered the first time she'd approached him. Her cheeks were red, her hands on her hips, and her eyes full of anger. She'd been beautiful. His little seven-year-old mind had gone blank.

She'd come to her sister's defense after some of the boys he'd been playing ball with had accidentally hit Abby in the ankle. Iian had been the leader of the pack and had received quite the tongue lashing from Allison. He remembered he'd apologized to Abby in front of his friends, never once taking his eyes off Allison. The apology had labeled him a wimp in the eyes of the gang of seven-year-old boys. And so, after making a fool of himself in front of everyone that day, he'd pretty much tried to ignore her for the next ten years or so.

In his teens, he'd stumbled through inviting her to their school dance, his voice cracking a half dozen times, but the final results were worth it. They'd gone to the dance and had ended the night with a perfect chaste kiss. The next day Allison's father had died of a stroke and she had backed away from him. He'd let her go then with a promise to himself that if he ever got another chance, he would never let her go again.

It was around nine the next morning when he walked into the hospital with his sister and sister-in-law, Megan. When everyone was saying their 'Hello's', he looked across the room at Allison and noticed that she was built like most models, tall and slender. However, now she looked too thin and pale, there were dark circles under her deep blue eyes. Her blonde hair, which had been very short the last time he'd seen her, was now longer and pulled back. He knew she had freckles on her nose and a slight dimple in her right cheek when she smiled. He was so glad she was home.

Allison had spent the rest of the night in the uncomfortable chair sitting next to her mother's bed. Her thoughts had wandered from her mother to her father, then to the last time, she had been in this hospital. When her sister, Abby, had died.

Abby and Ally had been as closest as two sisters could have been without being twins. They were both dusty blondes with deep blue eyes and were tall and curvy, so unlike their mother, who was shorter and had dark curly hair.

When they had lost their father, the sisters had banded together and taken over the management of the family's small antique store. They'd worked there after school every day. They even spent all their long hours of every warm summer inside, instead of running around like normal teenage girls should have. All for the sake of family.

Then a few years later, they had gotten news that Abby had Lymphoma. The cancer had spread so quickly that she was gone within months of her diagnosis before she had even turned sixteen.

Their mother took to spending most of her days on the couch and Allison was left to fend for herself. Adam's Antiques had sat on Main Street and had been her father's passion. She'd struggled the first year alone, trying to figure out how to run a business and a household had been hard. Finally, she'd found her balance.

She'd put her desires in the closet for the first two years after her sister's death. Never once going out on a date or focusing on herself, instead she had focused on her family business and silently painted in the back room. But one day that had all changed, the day she had met Megan, she had her to thank for launching her art career. Something she could never repay her friend for.

Allison had felt something pulling her back to the

small town of Pride, lately. She'd woken up in a cold sweat one-day last week, and it had only taken her a day to pack the essentials in her plush Los Angeles apartment. She'd cleared her schedule and left. She just knew it was time to come home.

Now when she looked up and saw her two friends walking into the room, she smiled. When she saw Iian trailing behind them, her heart jumped. He looked like he would rather be anywhere but in the sterile environment and was immediately mesmerized by him. It had been hard to live almost her whole life with a crush on someone who pretty much ignored her. She felt plain and grimy from having slept in the hospital chair all night. She hadn't even gone home to shower, and for that matter was still wearing the clothes she'd left California in. She must look terrible.

She greeted her friends and updated them on her mother's condition. The doctors still hadn't told her anything more.

When Dr. Stevens walked in a few minutes later, she gave him her full attention.

"Allison, I'd like to talk to you privately." He nodded towards the hallway.

"No, please, they can be a part of this," she smiled at her friends, her honorary family.

"Well," he said, taking a seat across from Allison. "As you know there are a few things that we're concerned about. Your mother had a very high temperature, and her red blood cell count isn't what we want to see. We're running more tests and would like to keep her here for a few days." He said as he looked over the chart again. "I know you answered this question last night, but has she been taking any medications that you're aware of?"

"No, um, I think she had some blood pressure medicine, but I'm not sure what it is."

"That's fine," he said as he wrote something down. Just then Allison looked up and saw her mother looking back at her.

"Mom!" she rushed to the side of the bed. "How are you feeling?" Dr. Stevens walked over and started checking her mother's vitals.

"Allison? Where am I? What happened?" She looked around the room at all the faces.

"You're at the hospital in Edgeview. I came home, and you had a fever," she said sitting next to her mother as she held her frail hand.

"Take it easy, Mrs. Adams. Just lie back. I'm Dr. Stevens. How are you feeling?"

"I don't know. Can I go home? I don't want to be here."

"Mom, they want to keep you a few more nights. How long have you been sick?" Allison could tell something wasn't right. Her mother's eyes kept darting around the room.

After the long silence, Allison asked again. "Mom?"

"Oh Abby," she patted her hand. "I was just dreaming about you, I'm so glad you're here. Your father was getting worried, you know we don't like it when you sneak out at night."

She laid her hand on Allison's cheek, which had gone very pale.

Iian stood once again on his hill, looking over the town of

Pride. He often came out here to think or take long walks along the shore to clear his head. He could make out a stream of smoke coming from the Adams' chimney and wondered how they were doing.

It had been a few days since the trip to the hospital. Alzheimer's was a hard blow and he knew that Allison had been very busy since returning home.

Lacey, Megan, and a group of church women had been helping her out. He'd even helped by making a big batch of his own chili, which he had his sister deliver instead of taking it there himself. It wasn't that he was avoiding seeing her again. He just thought that she had a lot on her mind and he didn't want to get in her way. His sister, on the other hand, had scolded him for not being more neighborly. But she'd delivered the chili and left the subject alone, Iian thought she knew about his secret crush on Allison.

Looking up, he remembered seeing Allison in the grocery store yesterday. She'd been alone and had been cornered by a dozen of the older women in town, which in his mind, accounted for half the population in Pride. Once he'd stepped into the building and given his sternest look towards the group, the women had dispersed. Allison had left without a glance in his direction.

As he stood looking out at the vast ocean spread before him, he realized that he was lonely. He'd been living in his large house for almost two years by himself. Sure, he had kept himself busy at the restaurant most days, and then there were the family dinners every week. Looking back, he couldn't remember the last time he had been out on a date. He'd tried dating after his accident, but it always left him feeling frustrated with the lack of ability to communicate.

Because of the communication issues, he'd hand-picked most of his staff in the kitchen at the Golden Oar. Two of the other chefs knew sign language, and the other one was quickly picking it up. Lacey was still in charge when it came to the dining room staff, and he let her be. The kitchen was his place, and looking over the town he realized, so was Pride.

His brother and sister now had their own families, which were getting bigger. Everything seemed to be changing without him. Since things were changing, it was about time he stood up and grabbed what he wanted before it was too late, and he figured he might as well start tonight after work.

"Come on Mama. Would you like to get out of this old house and have a real dinner?" It had taken some adjusting, but Allison had fallen into a pattern the last few weeks since she'd returned home.

The first couple of days home had been a blur. They had seen several specialists in Edgeview and they had also seen Dr. Stevens regularly. Once the news had spread throughout the small community, everyone within two counties had stopped by and delivered dish after dish of food. Some women had even come and cleaned the house for them. She felt that everything was falling into order.

The medications appeared to be working to regulate her mother's basic health issues, and Allison was finding her own pattern with her mother's Alzheimer's episodes.

Still, she hadn't gotten a good night's rest since arriving home. Her mother tended to wake at odd hours to do the strangest things like cooking or laundry. It had gotten so strange, that Allison didn't feel comfortable falling asleep without one ear tuned in to the hallway, just in case.

She still felt tightness in her chest every time her mother called her Abby, but it didn't shock her as much anymore.

Allison usually enjoyed getting out and decided today on a whim that they would go down to see Lacey at the Golden Oar.

Her mother, however, was not cooperating. Allison had laid out her mother's best slacks and a green silk shirt that she knew her mother loved. It was becoming more like she was babysitting a child instead of a full-grown adult. Her mother's moods were sporadic, and occasionally, Allison wished for help.

She walked over to the bed where her mother sat in her sweats and a large t-shirt. She sat down and pulled her mother's hand into her own and said, "Mom?" Her mother's eyes darted back to her face and blinked. "Do you want to go out?"

"Yes, dear, that would be nice. Shall we get ready?"

Half an hour later as they sat in front of the Golden Oar, her mother refused to leave her truck.

"If you think I'm going in there, you'd better think twice. People will see me! I look a mess," she said as she patted her hair, which Allison had washed and curled for her earlier that day. Allison noticed it could use a trim, but other than that, she thought her mother looked very nice. Her clothes were even pressed and tidy. She watched her mother run a hand over her slacks and wondered what she was upset about.

"Mom, we got all dressed up to have dinner. Do you want to go home instead? You look fine." She leaned over and flipped down the sun visor and showed her mother the small mirror.

Her mother patted her hair again, and then reached down and pulled some lipstick out of her purse. She applied it with even, quick strokes, snapped the lid back on, then flipped the visor up.

"There, now I'm presentable. Well, come on, I'm starving." Her mother smiled over at her.

Iian had been making his usual rounds in the dining hall to make sure everything was moving smoothly. He enjoyed the people of his town; for the most part, he could communicate with most of them pretty well.

Currently, he was sitting at a table with Jenny and Lori. The two friends had decided to have a girls' night out and had gone through several margaritas each. He'd gone to school with the pair and he'd even tried dating them in the past, but communication had been an issue. Now they were just good friends. Conversations were slow-going when he had to read lips and since he didn't like speaking, due to how unsure he was about his voice. But, he knew that it was a part of who he was now. After all, not everyone knew sign language.

Iian thought that the women were quickly on their way to becoming drunk. He had been trying to fend off Jenny's advances when he felt a familiar pull. He couldn't explain it, but he knew that Allison was about to walk into the restaurant a second before she did. He glanced over at the door and waited.

∼

The restaurant had never looked or smelled so good in her whole life. The large dining room was still beautiful, it's tall windows overlooked the ocean and the boat docks of Pride. Looking out the large windows at the sunset over the Pacific, she thought the restaurant still had the best views in town. The cherry wood of the dining tables and the hardwood floors gleamed. However, it was the paintings that hung on each wall that had always held her full attention. Iian's grandmother had painted everyone over eighty years ago, and every single one was a masterpiece.

She'd spent a good deal of her childhood here and remembered feeling like it had always been a part of her. After all, she'd gotten her first glimpse of what she had wanted to do in life here. The creative artwork had opened a door in her mind. One of her earliest memories was sitting at the back table with her family and trying to copy the beautiful mermaid painting that hung over the fireplace. Looking up now she smiled, seeing the painting was still in place.

As they were seated, she noticed Iian sitting at a table with two women. She thought how typical it was of him to be surrounded by women, one was hanging off him and Iian actually appeared to be enjoying it. As she looked at him, he glanced over and just smiled at her with one of his sexy, lopsided grins.

When he flashed it reminded her of the dance they'd

gone to in junior high. She could have sworn that there was a connection there, but he never called her back after. She'd chalked it up to him not being interested. She kind of felt broken-hearted. After that, he'd flaunted around town with almost every cheerleader at the small school, at least he had until his accident.

Trying to ignore him and his sexy smile, she took a seat next to her mother, two tables down from the group. She still thought of him as a good friend though, it's just that she'd always hoped for something more. He'd made it very clear to her that he wasn't interested in her that way. Oh, he didn't say so, she could just tell from the way he treated her.

Trying to focus on the now she asked, "What are you going to have, mom?" Allison looked over the menu. "Everything looks so good."

Her mother was studying the menu as well. "Hmm."

"I can recommend the lemon halibut in white wine sauce or the steak with portobello mushrooms. How are you ladies doing tonight?" The question was from Iian who stood behind her mother looking very tense.

It shocked her to hear the richness of his voice, she didn't realize she'd missed the sound. The last words he had spoken to her had been so long ago.

When she looked up at him, her heart almost jumped out of her chest. Iian was not only tall and muscular, but he had added some muscles since the last time she'd been in town. His waist was narrow and the rest of him looked very good in dark blue jeans that were a little worn. He had on black boots and a white chef's button-up shirt that, she noted with pleasure, strained around his biceps. His hair was a little longer, but he still had the jet-black curls

23

that she always loved. His face was strong and there was a little cleft in his chin. She really liked that little cleft. He had a cocky smile on his face as he watched her scope him out.

"We're doing okay. Would you like to sit?" She asked gesturing towards the empty chair next to her mother. He nodded his head and took a seat and gave her a big smile that had her toes going numb.

Her mother fluffed up her hair and said, "Oh, hello Todd. How's your father?"

Allison's cheeks turned red a little, and she said, "No, mom, this is Iian, Todd's brother, remember?"

Iian noticed her flush cheeks, but since he'd been looking at her mother, he wasn't sure what had been said. He did understand what Allison had said, so he looked over at Mrs. Adams.

"Hello, Mrs. Adams. How lovely you look this evening."

"Oh, well, you Jordan boys are all very handsome men. Don't you think so, Allison dear?" Her mother smiled at Iian.

He watched as Allison's flush deepened and his smile widened even further. It had been years since he allowed himself to speak in front of her. He thought it would make him feel awkward, however, it had actually had the opposite effect. Seeing her blushing face, allowed him to relax back in the chair and continue his conversation with the two women. Maybe it was the fact that he was on his turf, he didn't know but it seemed that while he started to relax,

Allison started to get on edge. He realized he enjoyed watching her blush and especially liked it when she bit her bottom lip, which made it hard to read them instead of wanting to kiss them.

"Is Lacey working tonight?" Allison asked nervously.

"No, she keeps showing up, but I send her home."

"Your sister has been helping us out the last couple weeks. I always did enjoy having her around," Mrs. Adams said as the waiter delivered their dishes.

Iian stood to excuse himself so they could enjoy their food. "Yes, Lacey has always been very helpful. You will let me know if you need anything. Anything at all."

As he stood, he met Allison's eyes and was trapped in the richness of their blue color. "I better get back to the kitchen. Enjoy your dinner." Reaching over he placed a small kiss on her mother's hand.

"I'll see you around Ally."

Allison smiled as she realized she enjoyed her name coming from his lips. She had just enough courage to smile back at him as he turned and walked away.

I'll see you around Ally. Why had that sounded more like a threat? She wondered. She did like hearing her nickname come from his lips.

"Oh, well," her mother blushed as Iian moved back to the double doors. "Like I said, all good-looking men in that family. You know Abby, I had hoped that you and Todd would make a couple. Then he married Sara. Always was a homely little thing. I never liked her father, Mr. McKinley; he was a beast of a man. Oh, well." Her mother picked up her napkin and placed it neatly in her lap. She was becoming accustomed to being called her sisters name. "Now Mr. Jordan, that was a man. You know I never did tell you, girls, that George and I had been an item in high school," her mother sighed, "Yes, he was the one that got away." Then she picked up her fork and began eating.

Allison didn't know how much more of the emotional games she could handle. She loved her mother, but this disease was taking hold so fast it made her head spin. Adding to it was the news that her mother and Iian's father had been an item in school. She didn't know how many more surprises she could handle. She just prayed that her mother's good mood would last through the evening.

CHAPTER 3

$\mathcal{H}$alfway through their meal, her mother had become irritated at something. She still wasn't sure of what, but she could see the tension building in her face.

"Mom? Are you okay? Do you want to go home?" Allison leaned over to take her hand.

"Don't touch me!" Her mother snapped out loud enough that the whole restaurant looked over. The two women Iian had been sitting with earlier looked over, chuckled, and then bent their heads together. Allison was sure they were enjoying a good laugh at her expense.

"Mom," she whispered, reaching out to her again.

"Tell your father to go to hell. I don't care what he says, you can't go," her mother yelled and then jumped up from the table and started walking across the room quickly. Allison was two steps behind her when her mother ran right into Iian.

"Mrs. Adams is there something I can help you with?" He asked in a patient voice.

"Oh!" Her mother's fists were clenched by her side. She blinked a few times and then said, "Yes, would you be a dear and fetch my coat. I think I have a headache coming on and would like to go home."

Allison walked up behind with her jacket and purse in hand.

She mouthed, "I'm sorry," to Iian.

"Mrs. Adams, you come back soon and visit me." Iian helped her with her coat and then took her arm lightly and started walking towards the front door.

"Oh, you should come to visit us tomorrow. I can bake some of those cookies you boys always enjoyed. We haven't had company for weeks. Bob and I would be so happy to have you come over. Allison, wouldn't you like to see your little friend tomorrow?" She asked, patting Iian's hand like a two-year-old. It was quite funny to see her mother's five-foot-nine frame standing next to a six-and-a-half-foot man, calling him a "little friend".

"Yes, Mom, that sounds like fun." Allison chimed in trying to play along.

Once they had gotten her mother into the car, she turned around to faced Iian. She hadn't realized how close he was and felt intimidated at his height. She was tall herself, reaching almost six feet, but he towered over her.

Most men she'd dated were either her height or shorter. She had never really had to crane her neck to look at anyone like she was doing now. It was nice.

"You don't have to visit tomorrow. I'm sure she won't even remember dinner tonight." She tried to smile at him.

"I would very much like to visit. I've missed you since you've been away. Maybe we can catch up." Reaching up, he placed a strand of her hair behind her ear.

His closeness was intoxicating. All her nerves flooded back to her and she found it hard to concentrate on breathing.

"I can bring some lunch," he kept a strand of her hair in between his fingers lightly.

"Well..." She found it hard to think of what to say next. His eyes were on her lips; she quickly licked them and in turn looked at his mouth. It was a sexy mouth; his lips were full and he was smiling. She looked up into his eyes. She knew he was looking at her lips to read what she was saying, but there was something more in his eyes.

"See you tomorrow then. Around eleven?" When she nodded back, he quickly shoved his hands in his pockets and walked back through the front doors.

Her mouth was intoxicating. It had taken all his strength to pull his eyes away from her.

He felt like humming but just smiled to himself instead. It was nice to know that he could make her feel nervous. It had been there on her face. He thought he was always the one to be nervous around her and had never really focused on how she had been acting. Tonight, however, he had focused on her and only her. He enjoyed the feel of her hair in his hands and hoped to enjoy it again soon. He wanted to get his hands on her.

As he made his way back through the restaurant, Jenny and Lori waved him over again. He motioned to their waitress to cut them off, as Jenny was currently sitting on top of the table. After all, this was a family restaurant, not a bar.

"Jenny, Lori, I think you two have had enough tonight," he said with a smile as he walked over to pull Jenny off the table. He noticed she wasn't quite stable on her feet. "Why don't I call you a cab?"

"Oh, come on Iian, join our little party. We were just going to head over to Lori's place and sit in her hot tub. Why don't you come have some fun with us?" Jenny leaned on him and twirled his hair around her finger.

"Yeah, Iian come to play with us," Lori said, almost falling out of her chair with laughter.

Iian took a deep breath. Right then he would have chosen to be anywhere other than here. There had been a time in his life where he would have gladly played the game with these two. However, recently he had outgrown their games. As he untwisted Jenny's fingers from his scalp, he looked up to see his brother standing at the back of the room with a humorous grin on his face. Iian quickly signed for him to help get the girls under control. His brother smiled and signed that he was a married man now. Then he walked into the back room leaving Iian to fend the women off.

It took all his patience and almost fifteen minutes to get the intoxicated pair into a taxi heading home. More than once his butt had been grabbed by either woman. He was pretty sure one of them had left a small bruise on his right butt cheek. Once freed from their grasp, he stormed into the back towards his office. His brother sat with his feet up on the desk, looking over some papers.

Iian signed, "Way to help out, bro. I was being mauled out there, and all you can do was laugh," he pushed his brother's feet off his desk.

As Todd's feet hit the ground, he signed back. "Looked

to me like you had everything under control. Besides, I'm a married man. I can't have people seeing me being mauled by other women," he smiled and added, "Besides, we all know you enjoy being handled by those two. They come around often enough. By the way, which one is it this week. Jenny?" He laughed at Iian's crude reply, which would have been more appropriate coming from a sailor.

Iian sat down hard in his chair.

"Come on, those two have been after you since school. Either let them down gently or make up your mind which one you want."

Iian looking directly into his brother's face. "I have made up my mind."

"Who?"

"Allison Adams." At Iian's reply, Todd's chin dropped.

Just then one of the waitstaff poked his head in momentarily and said, "Todd, your pizzas are ready."

"Thanks." Turning back to his brother he signed, "So, you're finally going to go for her? All I can say is… It's about damn time!"

Iian stood and started pacing the small room in frustration. Then he turned on his brother and signed, "Don't start on me! She was here tonight with her mother." He chewed his bottom lip and remembered the lost look in both of their eyes. "Her mother isn't doing well. Ally is holding up though."

Todd saw the concern on his brother's face. Ever since he could remember, his brother had been mooning over one person. He knew there had been other women, but in his mind, Iian had always focused on one. Allison Adams.

As Todd got up and walked to the door, he turned and signed, "I'm sure you can handle Ally. I say go for it." He

31

smiled as he walked out the door to grab his dinner for his family.

Iian sat there and ran over the evening again in his mind. He asked himself if he had wasted every minute of his life. He'd spent years avoiding Ally because of his fears. He discovered after dinner tonight that he wasn't the only one who had been affected.

He was determined to start living a new life, one where he wasn't alone all the time, and there was no time like the present to start. He got up, and made an excuse to his staff, climbed onto his motorcycle, and headed toward that new life.

Allison was about to pull her hair out. After the wonderful dinner at the restaurant, her mother had insisted on finding the old cookie sheets. Ally had tossed them out years ago. To calm her mother down, she had spent almost ten minutes looking in every kitchen drawer and had come up with two newer pans that, according to her mother, *"just wouldn't do."* All along her mother chatted happily about having Allison's *"little"* friend over tomorrow and how the cookies wouldn't turn out properly if she didn't use the right sheets.

It seemed like a lifetime ago, but Allison missed the days when her mother had actually taken care of her. Allison felt she had always taken care of her mother since her father had died.

Her time alone in California had been spent painting, learning, or frequenting art shows. It had seemed to fly by more quickly.

She'd made quick friends with Ric Derby, owner of the Blue Spot Art Galleries. She had not only lived above the swanky gallery in the city but had also worked there part-time. Her art had taken off much quicker than she'd imagined. It had been in such high demand she felt like she was actually falling behind on keeping some of the deadlines she'd set for herself. She had been looking forward to coming home and relaxing, to taking a break from the busy life. She thought she wanted – no needed – the slower pace and some peace. She needed home.

It was at the last art show in San Diego that she'd decided to leave California for good. The feeling of the whole room staring at her had taken over. Sit was like being in an Alfred Hitchcock movie where the walls were closing in. She'd sprinted from the room and had ended up on the patio roof, hoping to be alone. Ric Derby, her boss, and friend, had apparently been feeling the pressure as well and had also escaped to the rooftop.

"It's a little stuffy in there. Come to get some air?" Ric smiled at her.

Their relationship had very quickly grown to a brother/sister friendship. She respected the man and admired that he kept a level head when dealing with all the "moody" artists, as he liked to call them. He had assured her that he never thought of her in that way or a romantic way. Actually, he made a point to tell her often how level-headed she was.

"I think I actually saw the walls moving in on me."

"Like in Star Wars?" He smiled at her.

"I'm sorry?" She leaned against the railing and tried to see the stars through the hazy night sky.

"You know the scene where they're rescuing Princess Leah and they jump in the trash, then the walls..."

"Close in on them..." she laughed. "Yes, much like that. Maybe I need a break?" She meant to think it but had said it out loud.

"So, take one." He smiled and took another sip of his drink.

Could it be that simple? She'd tilted her head, so she could keep trying to scan the night sky for stars. Finally, he turned around to face the same way.

"What are you looking for?" He looked up.

The clear night was just too bright from the city lights to see any stars. She took a large breath, released it, and realized what she really needed. Home.

As she looked around the kitchen at the mess her mother was making, it made her heart and headache. She knew that she'd choose the messy kitchen over a room full of stuffy people any day.

Standing up, she dusted her slacks off and helped her mother reach the cookbook on the top shelf just as the doorbell rang.

When she opened the door, she saw Iian standing in the light of the front porch. Upon seeing her, he pulled the screen door opened himself and stepped in without an invitation.

"Um, hello Iian?" She stepped back as he walked in. She didn't know why he was there, but a part of her was very glad he was.

"Are you okay?" he asked, looking around before she could answer. When his eyes returned to her face she nodded. "Where is your mother?"

"In the kitchen," she said, feeling dazed.

"Is everything alright?"

"Iian, she wants to bake cookies, and well..." she trailed off when his finger rubbed gently over her cheek. She hadn't been aware of the tears spilling down. "I just don't know what to do," she whispered.

"Well, I guess it's a good thing I showed up," she looked at him blankly, "Baking just happens to be my specialty." He gave her a lop-sided smile and pulled her back towards the kitchen.

Allison didn't quite know how it had happened. She stood and watched Iian work his magic around her small kitchen her mother sat at the table and chatted happily. Her mother had been so excited to see a man baking cookies in her kitchen that she started talking about the old days as if they were old and not current events. Things looked brighter with him moving around the small room.

Allison kept trying to help him out, but he was a whiz and she felt more in the way than anything. By the time he had put a batch of home-made chocolate chip cookies in the oven, her mother's head was drooping.

"Well dears, I'm going to head to bed. Goodnight. Oh, and save some of those for your little friend tomorrow." With that, she disappeared down the hallway.

When Iian turned, he watched her mother heading down the hall. He looked over at her with a look of question.

"She's going to bed," she signed to him. She rubbed her forehead with her hand. Her head was pounding, and she was sure she was going to have another sleepless night worrying about her mother.

~

Iian was shocked. Allison had signed the last statement with ease. He hadn't known that she knew sign language. There were a few dozen questions he wanted to ask her, but she was rubbing her forehead like she was trying to take the skin off. He saw her eyes dim and could see tears beginning behind her eyes.

Walking around her, he started rubbing her shoulders. He could feel her initial shock, but then she relaxed into his hands.

"You really should take a break; you haven't stopped since you got back." He could feel her body vibrate in his hands but didn't stop her to say that he couldn't see her lips. When he felt the vibration under his fingers stop, he added. "You didn't tell me you knew sign language." He felt her shoulders tense.

She slowly turned around and stood straight-backed. Looking into his eyes, she signed, "I learned it a while ago."

Then she turned and walked to the oven and peeked in. He waited. He could see the flush in her face and was interested in learning more.

When she finally turned around he asked, "What is a while?" He started to walk towards her.

His mind quickly replayed all the days he had signed something to one of his siblings in front of her. Conversations that he had hoped would remain private. The personalized and intimate sign motions he'd used to signify her name. He cringed inwardly.

Placing both his hands on the countertop on either side of her, he boxed her in and looked deep into her blue eyes. Had she purposely kept this from him? Did she know how he felt about her?

"How long?" He whispered. Because he needed it, he reached up and took her face in his hands.

∼

She felt as if he was stalking her. She could have sworn he moved like a large cat prowling towards prey. He had neatly backed her into the corner near the stove. Their eyes locked and held. She raised and lowered her shoulders for an answer.

She couldn't breathe. She could feel the heat from his body. She looked into his silvery eyes and was sure she had lost all coherent thought.

The week after his accident, her sister Abby had died. And since she'd spent a lot of time alone, she'd decided to teach herself sign language. She'd checked out every book in the library on the subject over the next few years. She felt funny about using the language with him, in case he wondered where and why she'd learned it. She didn't want to admit that it was because of him that she'd taught herself. So, she kept her secret and silently wished she could use it one day.

"Months after your accident," she revealed everything by those words. What would he think of her? Would he think she was as pathetic as she felt?

When her words left her lips, he swooped in and took her mouth.

It wasn't the first time Iian had kissed her, but it felt like it. This was so much different from the sweet kisses he'd given her years ago, or the friendly one he'd given her on New Year's a few years back. This was different, he was different, and she revealed in the differences.

37

His lips were hot on hers. When she hoped he would go deeper, he pulled back. She opened her eyes and looked at him. He was a breath away. She glanced down at his mouth and ran her tongue on her bottom lip and tasted him. Then he was kissing her again. She reached around and ran her fingers in his thick hair, holding him close. She enjoyed the silky soft curls, wrapping them gently around her fingers. She moaned as his hands played on her back.

She couldn't stop shaking. She felt warmth all the way down to her toes. Had any other kiss ever taken her so deeply? If so, they paled in comparison. She ran her hands down his neck, his shoulders, and finally reached his arms. She enjoyed the play of his muscles as she touched him.

This was Iian, the boy she'd dreamed about for half of her life. The man who had become her every desire.

His taste was intoxicating. He felt better than she had imagined over the years. His hands were on her hips as he pulled her closer, pulling her up so she could sit on the edge of the countertop. She wrapped her legs around him and held on as he ran his hands up and down her back slowly.

Allison heard a high pitch ringing in her head and pulled away. Placing her hands on his chest, she looked over at the stove timer, then back at his questioning face.

The cookies are done," she said, pulling away.

CHAPTER 4

hree hours of waiting in a doctor's office in Portland's hospital was quite enough. Her mother sat across from her dressed in a thin paper robe, which had been designed by someone centuries ago to give doctors the ease of looking at a patient. However, it wasn't designed to keep them warm in an all-too-cold office. One that the doctors and nurses claim was kept at a normal temperature.

After talking to three nurses and finally seeing the head nurse to complain of the wait and the cold, which her mother had to suffer, Allison hustled her mother into her warm jacket and out of the office.

"*'Go to a specialist in Portland'*, they said, '*Maybe they can give you better news*' they said. Well, that was a terrible waste of time," she complained as they drove back to Pride with the heat in her car at full blast. She was very concerned that her mother might have just caught another cold waiting for the "*Specialist*" to tell her the same news that the last one had told her.

Now she had a headache and feared she too had caught something at the doctor's office. Just when they reached the house, the rain started. Springtime on the Oregon coast was unpredictable but often enjoyable. That is if you hadn't wasted hours sitting in a cold doctor's office.

Swearing off all doctors and medical people alike, she helped her mother into the house through the heavy rain. She'd had enough of sterile rooms and scrub-wearing good-willed people. All she wanted now was a hot bath and a glass of wine.

But when she walked in she noticed there were three messages on her voicemail.

Ric Derby, her boss "so to speak" had called and was the most important call to return. It seemed he wanted to do another art show highlighting her work, this time in New York. Which meant another deadline for more pieces. Knowing she'd have to fit some time in, she grimaced at the urgency in his voice. After all, she'd practically lived with the man for the last two years. Well, okay, she'd lived above the man.

He'd been her boss, art mentor, art dealer, and friend all in one. Everyone had assumed they'd been an item.

Then there had been a call from her agent, Steven Hill. The man was a shark, and he was out for blood. If there was a deadline, he wanted it done two weeks sooner. She couldn't complain though. Because of him, her art was selling for six figures now.

The last had been a call from Paris. She'd filled out the paperwork to attend art school there before she'd left California. It appeared they had received her application and had some questions.

Rubbing her head, she thought of all the changes in her life since she'd arrived home. No longer did she think about rushing off to Pairs to be a student. Or flying off to New York for an art show. All she could think about now was how she was going to root herself back into this tiny community, so she could take care of her mother.

Being honest with herself, she didn't want to leave Pride again. These people were her home, they were her reason for staying sane. No one in New York or Paris could ever fill the shoes of the people in Pride. Everyone had stepped up and helped her so much the last few weeks, that the thought of not having that support system would crush her.

The question was, how could she make her life here more of what she wanted it to be?

After returning her calls, she grabbed her pad and pencil and decided to get away for a while. She noticed the rain had lightened up and decided to take a short walk into town.

She sat across from the library under an overhang and started sketching the Town Hall. The building had sat in the middle of the square for close to two hundred years. Halfway through sketching the old building, she saw Patty O'Neil in front of O'Neil Groceries. The large woman had on one of her usual flowered dresses and yellow rain boots. She was sweeping the walk under the awning in front of her store with vigor.

Flipping the page, she started to sketch what she saw. She loved the colors of the people in town. You could sit on a corner and never be bored with what you saw. It took her less than five minutes to get what she wanted. When she looked down at her sketch, she decided then and there that she would have to paint it.

Some of her sketches stayed sketches. Others she turned into oil, watercolors, or acrylic. She thought this one would look great in acrylic. Smiling at the progress and the way her shoulders were completely relaxed, she picked up her art bag and headed home.

Iian sat across from his brother-in-law the next morning. Aaron was dressed in his white doctor's jacket. He had his stethoscope draped around his neck.

He signed, "Everything going alright? How are the headaches?"

"Fine, fine. I hate these damn things. Can't I just get my medication without an exam every year?" He knew he didn't really need the pills, except once a month when the headaches got so bad he could hardly see. They were always brought on after a night of terrors and bad dreams. The memories kept trying to surface but seemed to always be pulled back into the darkness of his mind. This time it was so bad, he'd even hallucinated and thought he saw his father at the end of the hallway this morning.

"That bad huh?" Aaron wrote something down in his file. Iian thought he could read people very well since losing his hearing. His sister had the same uncanny knack for it. But Aaron's ability took the cake. The man always seemed to know just what was going on physically with him.

When Aaron turned back towards him, Iian gave him his favorite sign.

Aaron signed back. "Is that any way to talk to your favorite brother-in-law? If your sister were here…"

"God, please don't tell her I said that," he signed back. "Last week she overheard me cussing up a storm after stubbing my toe in my own damn shower. A man isn't even safe to speak in his own home." Looking over at Aaron, he continued. "I'm going to have you text me when she decides to run over to my place at the spur of the moment from now on. Did you know she yelled at me for leaving a beer can on the coffee table?"

He watched Aaron chuckle. Iian was rubbing his hands on his temple. Then he saw the light in his brothers-in-law's eyes and said, "Don't even think about it," Aaron had turned around to write something in his file. When he turned back, he signed.

"What?" Aaron tried to put on an innocent face. Iian wasn't buying it.

"Listen, bro. I don't want to be scanned, poked and examined at Edgeview or Portland. Last time I spent two hours freezing in that damn room while the doctor went out for a smoke," he rubbed his temples harder.

Last night had been a bad one. He was working on only two hours of sleep. All he needed was his damn headache prescription filled, hence the trip into his doctor.

Then Aaron pulled out his ace card.

"Iian, don't make me call your sister. She was going to stop by for lunch, but I'm sure she wouldn't mind taking an earlier lunch break. We'll just do a scan this time. No blood work, I promise."

Rubbing his forehead, a little harder, he decided he didn't have the energy to fight with anyone else today, let alone his sister.

"Fine, just set it up and text me the details. Can I get my prescription now? Before my head explodes?"

Three hours later, Iian sat behind his desk in his office and swore his head *was* going to explode any minute. Three of his staff members were out with the flu. He had just caught one of his new dishwashers stealing from the liquor supplies and had fired him. Now he was four staff members down for the day.

He had received a text from his sister about his appointment. It appeared Aaron had let the "boss" handle him after all. It took less than twenty messages before he was persuaded to keep the appointment. To top it all off, his sister had ended up showing up at his office door twenty minutes later. Of course, he had quickly put her to work. But since she was several months pregnant, he had her helping out at the bar. She started to complain, but then he explained that he had closed the bar due to being short-staffed.

He knew she was bored since she'd only been helping Megan out at the Bed and Breakfast for the past several weeks. He'd let her take over that task completely. At least he had after a talk with Aaron. Aaron's opinion was that it was easier on her, during her pregnancy, to help Megan than to come into the restaurant.

So he had doubled his efforts around the place to take up the slack. She still came in twice a week, but for the most part, the place was his. He enjoyed it and most days it *was* enjoyable. Today, however, with the lack of sleep and the headache, he wished Lacey would just take over for the rest of the day. He had a stack of bills that needed to be taken care of and he was having a hard time focusing his eyes through the pain.

Just then Thomas, one of his floor managers, walked in. Iian liked the man he was efficient, kind to customers, and according to some of the local women, not bad looking. Iian had hired him on the spot three years ago after learning he knew sign language and hadn't regretted it. In fact, just last year, he had moved him to floor manager.

"You'd better come out front," Thomas signed. "It's Kevin Williams again."

Damn it! Couldn't he get a break today? His head was pounding like a bitch in heat, and now he had to deal with the town drunk and bully.

Kevin had been two years older than Iian in school. He had been the varsity quarterback and the star pitcher. The all-out athlete had barely graduated high school before he'd gotten one of the cheerleaders in his class pregnant. Three kids later, he worked at the mill across the river and lived in a broken-down trailer somewhere outside of town. The man hunted, fished, and pretty much killed anything that moved with his vast collection of guns and knives. He's what most people called a survivalist. Iian called him just plain crazy, only because he knew the man. Kevin was no survivalist. He was a nut job who liked to pick on anything smaller than he was. Iian had outgrown that criteria in the fifth grade. Brenda, Kevin's wife sometimes stayed at her friend's house in town sometimes with the kids, sometimes alone. The whole town assumed the reason his marriage was on the rocks was due to abuse.

Since the Golden Oar was one of the last remaining places with a bar in town, beside Barley's pool hall at the edge of Main Street, Kevin darkened the doors fairly often. Usually when he'd been kicked out of Barleys. Every time he ended up here, he'd caused problems. On several occasions, Iian or one of the staff had to call the local police.

Iian wasn't in the mood to deal with Kevin right now, drunk or not drunk.

Walking through the double swinging doors that led to the large dining hall, Iian could tell this time could be bad. Turning back to Thomas, he signed, "Go ahead and give Robert a call."

Not waiting for a reply, he walked into the room knowing Thomas would make the call to the Sheriff.

When he was halfway across the room, he saw Lacey struggling to deal with the man. His sister stood five foot four Kevin was a little over six feet and had a good hundred and fifty pounds on his petite sister. He couldn't tell what was being said, as the man's back was to him.

Speeding up, he was just short of them when he saw Kevin reach across the bar and grab his sister's arm.

"You'd better remove that hand from my sister, before I remove it for you," Iian spoke. Years of not speaking a lot didn't diminish the tone in which he chose to say the words. He may be out of practice, but he knew he had put enough behind his words to have the man afraid because Kevin's hand quickly dropped to his side as he spun around to face Iian.

"We've already called Robert, so you might as well take a seat on that stool," Iian pointed to the end of the bar, "and wait until he gets here." Turning to his sister, he signed. "Are you alright?"

"Yes, I'm fine. He's drunk and wanted another beer," she signed back rubbing her arm where the man had grabbed her. She stopped when apparently Kevin spoke to her. Turning his head quickly he glared at Kevin, who was now sitting on the bar stool.

Turning back to his sister, he saw the flash of humor in her eyes. "He really is afraid of you," she signed back to him, "He came in drunk about ten minutes after I got here. Put back three beers and that's when I cut him off."

"Well, he's leaving now" Iian spoke out loud since he'd just seen the sheriff's car arrive out front.

"Don't come in here drunk again, Kevin," he said as Robert walked in the front door. "Robert, can you take Kevin home, since he's overstayed his welcome?"

"Sure thing, Iian," Robert said, taking a hold of Kevin's arm as the man struggled to stand from the stool. They walked towards the door.

Lacey overheard what was said next and thought it better to keep it from her brother.

"Damn Jordan family, always thinking they're better than me. And Iian is the worst one day I'd like to…" and the door shut out the rest.

Iian signed, "You're going home. Get your coat." He walked away without giving her a chance to argue. Lacey quickly caught up with him as he entered the back room.

"Now just wait a minute," she signed after jumping in front of him. "You are not the boss of me, Iian Conner Jordan. I will go home when I'm ready to go home and not a minute sooner."

Deciding two could play at this game, he signed back. "Don't make me text Aaron. Because you know I have him on speed text." He started to pull his phone from his pocket.

The look on his sister's face told him he'd won this

argument. Funny, in his whole life, he thought that this was the first time he'd ever done so.

After he made sure his sister left safely, he stalked back to his office. He knew he needed to start working on the pile of bills and orders. Instead, he sat there and thought about his life.

The pills had finally kicked in around six that night, so the rest of the evening had been a blur. It's not that the medicine dulled him, but he always felt less aware of everything when he took them.

Working and living in a small town, he wanted to keep some things private. Knowing this couldn't happen in a small town, he'd been tagged as being somewhat of a loner.

Actually, at seventeen he'd been viewed quite differently. It had been one of the highest points in his life. He had several girls in town that he was seeing and he was working at the restaurant with spare money in his pocket. Then there had been his 1962 Dodge Dart that was sitting in the garage that he was turning into a sweet cherry of a ride. He'd made plans to go to California after school to attend one of the highest-rated culinary schools. Things had definitely been looking up for his future.

The weekend of his eighteenth birthday had arrived and his father had pulled him aside after dinner one night. A birthday sail with his old man had been the last thing he'd wanted to do. Iian had actually made other plans with Stacie Roberts, a high school cheerleader, who had been trying for years to get his attention. Well, he figured it was about time he gave it to her.

But his dad had been stubborn, so he'd called off his

plans and instead spent it on a small sailboat with his old man.

He'd woken up almost a week later in the hospital with several broken ribs, cuts all over his body, and a nasty bump on his head. The worst part was the loss of his father and the knowledge that he would never hear again.

He had little to no memory of what had taken place in the water. The last thing he did remember was leaving the dock. His dad had smiled over at him as he stood at the helm of the tiny vessel. That memory was frozen in his mind, much like a snapshot. Which kept coming back to him at the oddest times.

It had taken him almost three years to get back onto a boat, and even then, he'd only gone as far as five miles offshore. It irritated him that he still had problems sailing. He'd been raised on the water, he loved the ocean. Now his hands would get sweaty, his breath would come in harsh gasps, and his mind would fog up. Funny, he felt the same way when he saw Allison.

The doctors called it post-traumatic stress syndrome. He called it, and himself, just plain stupid. He hated that he could lose control of his own body so easily.

After being raised on the water during the first part of his life, he sometimes missed the feel of the open ocean. He'd finally gotten himself to the point where he could control the shaking for short periods of time. But he still couldn't control himself when he saw Allison.

Now he didn't feel comfortable speaking in front of most people, just his family. A family which it seemed was getting larger every day. Todd and Megan had their two children, Matthew and Sara. And then his sister Lacey and Aaron's baby was due in a few months.

He realized he was the only one without someone to go home to… yet.

At a quarter to one in the morning, Iian walked into his empty house. The place was dark except for the hall light upstairs, which had always been left on since he was a small child when he'd been afraid of the dark. As a grown man, he had left it on out of habit.

He loved the house he grew up in, but now, as the only inhabitant, he found it lonely and way too large for one person. His brother's and sister's rooms had sat pretty much untouched since they'd moved out. His father's room sat behind closed, large double doors, untouched since his death over ten years ago.

Iian's small room was still decorated from his youth. Basketball paraphernalia lined every wall. A large poster of Michael Jordan hung over his bed. For the most part, when he had company over, especially women, he made a point to not let them stay the night. In fact, he'd never had an overnight guest.

It wasn't that he was cold or heartless, he just liked his space. Losing his hearing had pretty much taken the choice of intimacy from him, or so he thought. Most people in town didn't know sign language, and most girls he dated didn't care if they had a deep and meaningful conversation. Up to this point, he had been okay with that.

As far back as he could remember, he had only really thought of one person in that way.

Shutting the front door behind him, he flipped the lock and switched on the stair lights. Looking around the empty entryway, he guessed it was about time he started thinking about fixing up the place. It had been his solely for almost two years. The three siblings owned the large house together, but everyone knew it was his.

The downstairs had been redecorated a few years back, thanks to his sister. The newer appliances still shined in the remodeled gourmet kitchen. The huge fifty-two-inch flat-panel television hung on the den wall with large brown leather couches and chairs positioned around for the best view. The coffee tables and end tables gleamed with newness.

Lacey had overseen replacing the old carpet in most of the downstairs rooms with dark hardwood flooring, right before he'd graduated high school. His father's office, which had been used by Todd when he had lived there, now housed his own laptop, papers, and books.

The back room, which had been an old sewing room his mother had used before his birth, was now a home gym. His weights and treadmill sat facing a wall of mirrors. Todd still came over some days and used them.

Taking the steps two at a time, he stopped at the end of the long hallway and swore he could see his father standing in front of the large double doors again.

He shook his head and blinked several times and looked again at the empty doorway. The dark wood of the master-bedroom doors gleamed. He remembered running in them as a young boy and crawling into his father's giant bed after a nightmare.

To his right was his sister's bright pink rooms. She had the second-to-largest bedroom which had its own adjoining bathroom. To his left was his and Todd's rooms. There was a good size bathroom between the two smaller rooms. Todd's old room was the closest to the stairs. His brother had re-decorated it after his first wife's death and it was the only room that was updated.

Iian walked down the hallway and gripped the brass door handles to his father's room. He had plans to change things, change his life, and the first hurdle he had to jump was behind these heavy doors. Taking a deep breath, he pushed them open and walked in knowing that these changes would help him obtain his deepest desire. Allison.

CHAPTER 5

*A*llison was enjoying herself for the first time since coming home. She was standing in the town's small library, talking to a friend. Her mother was across the room enjoying herself as she read a book.

Tanya had been a close friend in middle school, but after her parent's divorce, she had moved away to Portland. Since her own divorce seven years ago, she'd moved back to Pride and taken over as vice-principal of the elementary and middle schools.

There were twenty of her school children, all around the age of eleven, quietly sitting around the small library reading or finding books.

She enjoyed Tanya's company. Actually, it was funny to look at the pair of them. Where Allison was tall and had a fair complexion with light blue eyes and fly-away blond hair, Tanya was her complete opposite. She was shorter, around five-six, and her curves had always made Allison jealous. Her darker skin and thick black hair marked her Indian heritage.

"It's so wonderful that you're back to stay," Tanya was saying. Allison noticed that her friend's eyes wandered to a group of children that had gathered towards the back of the room. Snapping her fingers, her friend got the children's attention and they quietly dispersed from each other. "Actually, I wanted to tell you, I went to Portland a year back and saw some of your art in that gallery downtown. I have never seen anything more beautiful than the water-color you did of the shoreline. You know I think it's just terrible that you kept your wonderful talents hidden for so long."

"I didn't really keep them hidden away. I just didn't tell anyone in fear of what they would think." Allison was used to hearing this from the locals. "I love all things art, I always have. It just took Megan giving me the push to turn it into something more than a hobby."

"Actually, you're giving me an idea." Her friend ran her hand down her long dark braid. "Karen, our art teacher, has been thinking of breaking up some of her art classes. She teaches for all the elementary, middle, and junior high school kids. She's been begging me to get someone to take the younger kids off her hands, so she can focus on the older ones. Would you be interested in helping us out? It wouldn't be a full-time position, at least not to begin with. Art classes are only three days a week." Her friend chewed her lip, waiting.

"Well…," she said, looking across the room. Now there were two girls sitting at the desk next to her mother. She was happily reading a book to them both. Both girls smiled and laughed when her mother spoke in a deep character voice as she read a story to the pair.

This could be what she'd been looking for. A chance at

some normality. Something that would root her back into the town and give her the feeling of being needed.

Smiling to herself, she decided to take a chance.

"What exactly did you have in mind?"

Three hours later, Allison sat in the kitchen watching her mother make dinner. The house had been thoroughly cleaned since her arrival. It still shined, reminding her so much of her youth. Her mother had been a typical type "A" personality. Everything had its place, everything had to be spotless. Allison could remember her mother yelling at her and her sister on a particular evening shortly before her father's death. She and Abby had just arrived home from school, and their books and bags were supposed to go immediately to their rooms. This time, however, both girls had been so excited about their father being home from a long trip, they'd dropped them and ran straight to his open arms. The yelling her mother had done was one of the worst she could remember. Unknown to Allison, she had spent the whole day cleaning the house.

She watched as her mother moved around the kitchen with fluid movements in a dance she'd seen her do for years and years.

"Mom? What do you think about me teaching an art class at the middle school for a few days during the week?"

"Oh, that would be lovely. You were always good at drawing. Is that what you want to do dear?"

"I think it's something I would enjoy." Chewing her lip, she watched her mother put the milk in the cupboard. "Mother, you just put the milk in the cupboard."

Her mother stopped, looked at her and then opened the cupboard door. "Well, look at that!" Chuckling, she pulled the milk from the cupboard and placed it in the refrigerator. "I tell you, sometimes I'm just so scatter-brained."

"Tanya says that I would have to get my state teacher's credential. She says it's something I could easily study for," she said to her mother's back. Thinking about it, it started to sound really fun. Oh, sure, she could still do her art. Maybe even occasionally fly out for a show. After all, she would have the summer to do whatever she wanted. Taking this job wasn't because she was hurting for money. Her art had made her enough in the past two years that she didn't think she would have to worry about money ever again.

"Well, really!" Looking up she saw her mother standing at the sink.

"What's wrong, mama?" Allison started to get up and go to her.

"I'm so very upset at you two right now. I thought I taught you girls better than this." She turned and shook a hand towel at her. "Just where is your sister? No doubt hiding in her room. I suppose you're going to tell me you had nothing to do with this." Her mother tossed the hand towel on the table next to her. Thinking that her mother was upset that she'd left it on the countertop she tried to calm her down.

"Mom, I don't know what you're upset about. It's just your hand towel." Picking it up, she looked at it. It was an older towel, one she'd seen since her childhood, one that had seen better days. It was frayed at the ends and the pretty picture of flowers were so faded, she could hardly make them out.

"My hand towel? My hand towel! I would never have

such a ragged thing as that for a hand towel." Her mother stormed off towards her room.

Allison rubbed her temples and decided a glass of wine would help her get through the rest of the evening.

$\sim$

It had taken Iian a week, with his brother and Aaron's help, to clean out all four rooms upstairs. They'd dragged everything up to the attic for storage. With all the furniture cleared out, he could focus on painting and re-carpeting. The carpet guys were going to arrive next week, which left him only a few days to patch and paint the walls.

Lacey's old room was going to take the longest. The bright pink paint that had donned her walls for years needed so much work. He actually thought of putting siding up instead. Once he removed her barre and wall of mirrors, he had uncovered a large space that was still white. Deciding to go ahead with the paint, he knew it would take him at least three primer coats on the pink walls. This would allow him to paint them all the light yellow he'd planned. In this room, he'd decided to keep the light oak hardwood floors their father had installed years ago instead of carpeting over them. Which meant he needed to sand and stain it all.

He went to work sore the last few days but seeing the progress on the upstairs was worth it. Besides, he was probably sore from sleeping on the couch downstairs, since the upstairs was a mess. His father's room, which he had to start thinking of as his new room, was completely painted and ready for carpet. His old room was still gutted and would probably remain so since he was planning on working on that room last. Since Todd's old room was the room that needed the least work, he had just slapped a fresh coat of paint and would add new furniture after the carpet was in. All he needed now was someone to share the large place with and there was only one person he could think of that fit in the empty space.

It had taken Allison hours of studying to get up the nerve to go to the campus in Edgeview and take the state test. After the test, she had walked out wondering why she'd stressed herself out. She knew all the answers, every single one. Not only was she sure that she'd passed the exam, she began to feel like she had even aced it.

She'd talked to her neighbor, Mrs. Evans, about keeping an eye on her mother while she was out. Mrs. Evans had not only enjoyed the idea but had shown up with a big pan of coffee cake on the morning of her test.

Now over two weeks after being asked by Tanya to teach, Allison was nervous. It wasn't that she was afraid of the work. After all, she'd been painting or drawing for most of her life. What she was nervous about was standing in front of a small room of students. She had received her teacher's certificate in the mail less than a day ago.

It had taken almost an hour that morning for her to pick out her outfit, finally choosing a pair of simple black dress slacks and a sea green silk top. She had even taken the time to French braid her hair, which had grown out since the last time she'd gotten the urge to do a short spring chop.

As she looked across the faces of her new students, she

wondered if she had made the right choice. How could she have thought she could do something like this? She was an artist! She belonged in a back room somewhere painting, alone. Not in front of a class full of pig-tailed girls and runny-nosed boys that couldn't sit still for more than five seconds. How was she going to control twenty eleven-year-old kids?

"Hello everyone, I'm Allison Adams. I'm going to be your new art teacher." The kids all sat looking at her like she was made of glass. At least they weren't throwing things at her yet. Turning to the chalkboard, she used her colored chalk to quickly draw what she wanted. It took less than two minutes to have all the kids in the classroom laughing.

"This is a caricature." She pointed at the likeness of herself. "Can anyone tell me what makes this a caricature and not just a drawing of myself?"

The whole class sat in silence. Then when she thought no one would answer, a small boy in the back row raised his hand.

"Yes?" Looking at her seating chart, she saw his name. "Yes, Sean. What makes this a caricature instead of a likeness?"

All the other kids turned and looked at the small boy who had freckles that crossed every part of his nose. His face soon matched the redness of his curly hair.

He stood and said something Allison would never forget.

"It's a character because you drew it funny." All the kids laughed. Sean quickly sat down with his head hung in shame.

"Hold on class. Sean is right. Take a look." She

59

quickly walked to the end of the chalkboard and drew again, this time taking care to not accent her features comically.

"Can you see the differences?" The kids all just stared at her.

Then a little girl with blonde curly hair that was tied up in a tight ponytail raised her hand.

"Yes, Mckenna."

"How did you do that?" She asked.

"Years of practice. Now let me show you what makes these two different."

By the end of the hour, Allison had discovered a new love. The children in her class had not only shown her she could teach art, but they had shown her that life was fun. Since her return home, she'd been caught up in a whirl-wind of doctor meetings and her mother's moods. She had smiled and laughed more in the last hour than she had since returning home.

Walking into Tanya's office she had a huge smile on her face and her mind was made up. She was going to take the teaching job. She was going to be a middle school art teacher, she laughed inwardly.

Three days later, she thought really hard about backing down. Leaving the house had even become a task since her mother had another "episode," as she had started calling them. Thank goodness she had calmed down before Mrs. Evans had arrived. Then her car had acted up at the town's only stop sign, causing everyone who had been outside and downtown to look over at her after the loud backfire. Of course, she had stalled it trying to quickly leave. She had to wave off the old men who were approaching from their permanent residence of twenty-odd years, outside the old barbershop.

To add to her day, she had to spend more than five minutes getting the two Simmons sisters to stop arguing. They had been fighting over whether Jenny's painting of a flower was that of a daisy or if it was just a weed like Julie, the older of the twins, was saying it was.

She had enjoyed when Eric Everett had shown her his painting of his gray cat. It not only looked like a cat, but he'd actually listened to her instructions about how to draw the back legs and had done them correctly.

Allison had been debating whether she wanted to be a school art teacher or to go back to the city and deal with all the art critics she so desperately hated. She came to the conclusion that the kids were easier to deal with at this point in her life.

It had been a long day; her head ached, her feet ached, and her back ached. How could so many little kids cause so much destruction? By the end of the day, her art room had looked like a large tornado had pushed through it.

The weather had been nice and warm for days. However, now the light rain that was falling was nothing more than a burden to her.

Parking her car in the drive, she was looking forward to a nice hot bath, maybe a glass of wine. Turning the doorknob, she discovered the front door was locked. Taking out her keys, she unlocked the deadbolt. Only to have it snap locked again.

"Mother!" She could hear her on the other side of the door. "Mother, it's Allison," Turning her key again, she tried the door handle, it was locked. She unlocked it, just in time to hear the deadbolt lock again. Laughing to herself, she tried a fourth time, only to have it happen again.

"Mother! Let me in!" She wasn't finding this funny anymore. Every time she would unlock the deadbolt, the door handle would lock. Then when she unlocked the door handle, the deadbolt would be locked quickly.

"I know who you are. I've told you before, you can't have any of it," The deadbolt slid home again.

"Mother, please let me in. It's wet out here and I'm tired." When her mother didn't respond, she sat on the front steps, protected from the rain under the small overhang.

Pulling out her cell phone, she messaged the only person she knew could help calm her mother down.

Waiting for his reply seemed to take forever. Finally, he messaged, "I'll be right there."

Iian had the day off and since there were men at his house installing his new carpet, he'd decided to swing by Megan and Todd's place. He had made his famous chili earlier to take to their guests at the bed and breakfast. He enjoyed cooking meals for the guests and usually stayed on for lunch.

He liked visiting with Megan, but it was really the kids he came to see. He loved spending time playing with little Matthew and Sara. Matthew was a shy little thing around others, but Iian brought out the monster in him. He liked to wrestle in the yard and play with little cars or trucks he always bought for the boy.

Sara was his precious diamond, as he liked to call her.

Her chubby one-year-old cheeks just called out to be kissed and snuggled with. She giggled and smiled when he tickled her, and when he left for the day she gave him sloppy kisses that left a soft spot on his heart. So after enjoying another great visit with his family, he headed home to see how the progress was going.

Walking into the place just as the rain started, the smell hit him full force: paint, stain, and new carpet. Smiling to himself, he headed up the stairs. Looking into Todd's old room first, he saw the carpet was already done. The plush Berber floor and fresh off-white paint made the room look brand new. Seeing that his old bedroom was also done, he headed into his father's room. He really had to start thinking of it as his room, someday.

There were two guys picking up small carpet clippings. He could tell that they hadn't noticed him yet, so he stood in the door and just looked. The room was three times the size of his old bedroom. On one wall was a large archway leading into the master bathroom, which hadn't been used in years. The glass-walled shower sparkled since his sister had come over and cleaned it. It was the only job that they would let her do to help out since she was growing bigger every day. The marble double sinks his father had installed for his mother on their wedding day gleamed, as well. Megan had seen to cleaning the rest of the bathroom. Everything smelled and looked new.

Smiling to himself, he thought of asking Aaron and Todd to help him move the massive bed and the rest of his furniture back down tomorrow.

After the carpet crew left, he started bringing down some of the smaller stuff, himself including the air mattress he was going to use. He was standing in the empty master bedroom when he saw a movement out of the corner of his eyes and swore he smelled his father.

Just then his cell phone vibrated with a new message. Looking down, he grabbed it from his jeans and quickly looked back up towards the empty archway and shook his head. He needed one night of real sleep, he thought, as he looked at the text message from Allison.

Ten minutes later he pulled up in front of the Adams' house. Allison was sitting on the steps of the porch. Her eyes were pink and he could tell she was either about to cry or had been crying.

The steady spring rain had continued through dusk and a slight chill was now in the air. He could see her shivering as he walked up the path.

"Still can't get in the house?" He signed.

"I stopped trying. It's so frustrating. She was yelling at me like I was a stranger trying to break into my own house."

Helping her to stand up, he held onto her hand and felt her fingers were chilled. Walking over to the door he knocked.

"Mrs. Adams, it's Iian Jordan. Can I come in?" he looked over to Allison to gauge if there had been a reply. When she shook her head "no", he continued. "Mrs. Adams remember I'm deaf, I can't hear you. I just wanted to come in and see if…" The door swung open.

Her mother was in large gray sweatpants with a huge white tee-shirt. Her hair was a mess, and there were clothes thrown all over the living room, again.

"Oh, Iian," she stopped to primp her hair. "Well, if I knew you were coming, I would have made some of my cookies. Well, don't stand out there in the cold. You two kids had better come in."

Her mother was treating her like a stranger which only made her feel worse. Her headache had only gotten worse sitting out in the cold on the front porch. When she had seen Iian drive up, she had almost lost it and cried right there in front of him.

By the time she shuffled her mother into bed, she was sure she would need a half bottle of wine or a big bowl of mint chocolate chip ice cream to make her feel better.

Iian had stayed around and entertained her mother while she had picked up all her clothes. Her mother had thrown all over the living room, something she had been doing lately. Why she chose to do this was still a mystery to her. She was starting to think that she would hire someone to watch her full time. Mrs. Evans could only watch her for a few hours at a time. Maybe somebody else could watch out for her the rest of the time.

When she walked back into the living room, she saw him sitting on the couch, looking through an old photo album her mother had handed him earlier.

Walking over, she sat next to him. There on the pages were she and Abby on her father's old boat. Boating had always been a part of her life. Living on the coast, she had loved to go out for trips with her family. Sometimes they would spend weeks on the small sailboat they had owned.

Looking over at Iian, she signed, "Thank you for helping tonight."

"Don't mention it. I always did have a soft spot for your mom." He reached over and toyed with the ends of her braid. She tried hard not to purr like a cat, but the light contact helped ease her headache.

"You've got a bad headache?" He spoke this time. Her eyes had closed when he started to stroke her hair. He continued to rub her head and then he nudged her to turn her back towards him. "I bet it can be stressful dealing with a bunch of kids all day, then coming home to this." He kept talking as he made his way down her neck to her shoulders.

The tension he felt there was almost shocking. "I've been working on the house all week and sleeping on the downstairs couch. They just finished putting carpet in all the upstairs rooms today. It looks wonderful." He continued to talk about what he was doing around his place in hopes of helping her relax.

She moaned in pleasure as his warm fingers moved up and down her neck. He was talking, and she could tell he wasn't expecting her to answer him back. When she felt like she could just slide down the couch and fall asleep, she turned to him. Looking directly into his eyes, she leaned forward and kissed him. She had wanted to kiss him since he'd walked up to her on the front porch.

She had kissed Iian all of four times. The first time was when they were no more than children. The second was a chaste peck on New Year's. The third was a heated kiss over a hot stove. This kiss was unlike any before. The slowness of the sweet kiss lasted until she began to shake with want.

She tasted like spring. She felt better than he had imagined over the years. Taking his time, he savored every inch of her mouth. Her lips were softer than any others that had come before. Her taste, sweeter than anyone else. He could lose himself in her mouth, in her taste. He had waited years, a lifetime it seemed, and wanted to savor every moment, every feeling.

He was sure that if he could bottle up the essence of her, he would quickly become a millionaire. He ran his hands over her slender form, enjoying the slight curve of her hips. He slowly traced the lines as she clung tight to his shoulders.

When he started to pull back, she reached up and grabbed a handful of his hair to pull him back to her mouth. This time, she controlled the speed. He could feel her vibrating and knew she was moaning. He could feel her melting against him. He used his hands on her hips and pulled her closer. She was soft, so very thin, and he enjoyed the feel of her body next to his.

Finally, she pulled back and rested her head against his shoulder. Taking a big breath, he enjoyed the feel and smell of her.

When she walked him out to his car, he kissed her again. He could just stand here forever with her on the front walk, in the night air, with the sparkling stars overhead looking down on them. The rain had washed everything clean, the clouds had dissipated, and the stars were out lighting the whole sky. The night air was still crisp enough that it reminded you that you were alive. Holding her close, he thought the feel of her helped him feel alive as well.

It was late when he got back to the house. He was pumped. He couldn't explain it but being with Allison gave him the energy to spare. Instead of hitting the shower and bed, he headed back up to the large attic. He figured he would use the extra energy to bring a few things back downstairs from storage in the attic.

He spotted a large luggage box that he hadn't seen in years. He knew the precious items that lay inside since the trunk had been up in the attic forever. No one really opened the box. In fact, he thought the last time someone looked inside was when he was a kid looking for some chalk.

On this particular evening, however, he felt the need to go over and open the lid. His grandmother's painting supplies were neatly tucked away. A large wooden easel sat shattered in pieces that he thought could easily be put back together. Paint brushes and other art supplies were neatly tucked in individual boxes with labels. Oil paints that he thought might be dried and unusable were still in their packages unopened. There were canvases that sat lined up along the back of the large box.

Making a decision, he started to drag the heavy box towards the stairs.

CHAPTER 6

The day after her mother's little *lock the front door game*, she was back at the school enjoying one of her favorite groups of kids. Several of them were happily drawing the flower arrangement she had brought along with her. It was almost lunchtime when Megan stuck her head in her door.

Happy to see her friend, she rushed to grab the little girl struggling to get out of her arms. Sara was one of the happiest, chubbiest babies Allison had ever had the pleasure of handling. The girl was giggling and drooling and had her faithful bunny hanging from her chubby hands. She wore a light pink dress with ribbons down the front. Her blonde curly hair had matching ribbons. The small white sandals were almost falling off her tiny feet. Matthew was shyly standing behind his mother's side. He was dressed in khaki pants with a blue shirt and a small tie. His dark hair had a slight curl to it and she could see the Jordan cleft in his little chin, so much so that he looked like a smaller version of his daddy and uncle.

"Here's my favorite kids." She held onto the squirming girl. "What a great surprise!"

"We were just down here registering Matthew for preschool next year and thought we would stop by to see if you wanted to have some lunch with us."

"What a wonderful idea. We just have ten more minutes to go before the bell." She turned to the room and said, "Class, this is Miss Megan and her children Matthew and Sara. Please welcome them."

Her class behaved wonderfully and sent out a greeting.

"I can set these two up with some crayons. I've got paint jackets that they can wear so they don't mess up their pretty clothes."

Less than two minutes later, Megan, Matthew, and Sara sat at one of her classroom tables with the other kids drawing.

She thought that they had actually enjoyed their time. After the bell rang, it took her less than a minute to clear the tables and leave for lunch.

It was over lunch that Megan said something that bothered her.

"I don't mean to be a snoop, but I can't not say anything. You know my past, where I came from. What I came from." Megan looked to both of her kids who were happily eating next to her. "I'm concerned about one of your students. I only sat with him for a few minutes, but well, I know the signs."

"What are you talking about?" Allison was starting to be very worried. She knew Megan's past, the abuse she had suffered from her ex-husband. Did she think one of her students was being abused?

"Some of the things little Tommy Williams was

drawing concerned me." She looked over to her own son, who looked like his tired head would drop in his bowl of macaroni and cheese. "Allison, he was drawing dead animals. At that young of an age, boys should be drawing cars, trains, or trucks, not animals with their heads ripped off," she whispered.

"What? Was he drawing that? I know Kevin. His father is into hunting; he probably takes the boy with him. I'll have a talk with Tommy about what we should and shouldn't draw in class."

"Well, it's more than that." Megan hesitated.

"Megan, you can tell me anything. You know that."

"I think he is being abused," she blurted out.

When Allison just looked at her friend, she continued.

"There were marks on his arms, and some of the things he was saying about his sister concerned me. Well, I don't know what the school can do, but I think you should have someone look into it. At least keep a close eye on him and follow your own instincts." Megan leaned over and pulled a sleepy Sara into her lap.

"You know I never did like Kevin Williams. He was the star football and baseball player. The only sport he wasn't the star in was basketball. Your brother-in-law Iian took that role. But Kevin always acted like he was better than everyone else. He made fun of others, pushing the smaller kids around, and he cheated on his girlfriends. He actually asked me to a dance in junior high, when he'd been going out with someone else. That's the dance I went to with Iian." She smiled, remembering that night.

"I'm going to look into this Megan. The thought of any child being treated bad…" she stopped and took a deep breath for her friend's sake. "You know it hurts me knowing what you went through after you told me."

"I know," Megan reached over and patted her friend's arm.

"Thank you for telling me. I guess I've been too caught up in my new teaching role to notice some things."

Over the next few days, Allison watched the boy carefully. She also had his younger sister Susie in another class.

It was really what she saw in Susie that caused her to be in Tanya's office with a stack of their drawings and her own notes of items she wanted to point out.

The little girl's bruises and marks on her arms and legs were worse than her brother's. Her drawings told a different story than Tommy's. Where her brother's drawings were about animals and death, Susie's were filled with fear. More fear than a child of seven should have.

Oh, some of her kids drew monsters in the closets or hiding under their beds. Susie's monster was in every picture. When she painted flowers, there was a dark figure on the corner of the paper. When she watercolored the Easter Bunny, the figure was poised just behind it. She had even colored blue spots on the bunny, and when asked what the spots were, the girl replied, "The bunny had been bad and had been punished."

That was when Allison had made up her mind. It wasn't that she didn't trust Megan's opinion, she had just wanted to be sure before going to Tanya with something this life-changing.

Almost two hours later, Allison left her friend's office

feeling assured. After making her case with Tanya, her friend had called an emergency meeting with the children's other teachers. Some of them had voiced their concerns as well. Then they had called in the professionals, the Child Protection Services. And after relaying their concerns to them, Allison and the other teachers had left and allowed them to do what they needed.

On her drive home, she was so nervous and wondered if she'd done the right thing. She ended up driving to the shoreline instead of home. Pulling out her bag filled with paper and art supplies, she headed to a secluded spot along the beach to sketch away her worries.

He stood over the hot stove and watched his kitchen staff rush around him and realized that this was the reason he had chosen to be a chef. The sights and smells of a busy kitchen were so embedded in his brain as a wonderful thing, he'd never had the time to think any negative thoughts about it.

Since losing his hearing, all his other senses had heightened, but nothing compared to what his sense of smell had become. He could tell if something would taste by smelling it. Herbs and spices thrown together gave off a different smell and he could mix and match as he pleased with ease. Some of his recipes called for unorthodox herbs and seasons but everyone ended up being a masterpiece.

Sweat trickled down his back and his muscles screamed at him from the hard work he'd been doing at home. Still, he stood over the stove and created what he knew would be yet another great dish.

Things were looking up for him, the work at the house was almost done. His relationship with Allison was coming along slower than he wanted, but he knew her mother and a new job were taking priority right now in her life. He remembered the other night sitting on her front porch and smiled to himself as he finished one plate and started working on the next order.

A few days later, Allison was late leaving the school. It was her last day for the week and her classroom had been a mess. She couldn't really blame the kids since it had been her idea to work with clay that day. It had taken her almost an hour to clean up all the clay that the kids had smeared everywhere.

She'd heard from Tanya that both Tommy and Susie, along with their younger sister, had been removed from their home by the Child Protective Services.

It was hard for her to think that Kevin or Brenda would do anything to hurt their children. After all, she'd gone to school with both of them. Kevin had been the picture-perfect athlete back then. Brenda had been the head cheerleader and most popular girl in school. Of course, since high school, Allison hadn't really been close to either of them. Actually, she hadn't been close to them in school either.

She knew Kevin worked in the mill across the river. After graduation, he had taken to hunting as his main hobby or sport. He went everywhere in town in his camouflaged outfits. He even drove a large truck that had a roll bar and lights on it. Sometimes he would carry his four-wheeler in the back. It too was decked out in camouflage and she'd even seen his hunting guns strapped to the back.

Once, she'd seen him come back with a pile of deer in the back. He'd had a couple of other guys with him that time.

Allison knew Brenda was a stay-at-home mom. Actually, Allison had hardly seen her since school. When she'd seen her in the store a few times, she noticed how quiet she was. She'd changed so much since high school. She used to be the outgoing head cheerleader but now had become a timid mouse of a woman.

She was thinking about them as she walked out of the school building just as the sun was setting. She was halfway to her car when she heard a door slam and turned to watch Kevin storm out of his truck.

"You've got some nerve," he said, as he stopped right in front on her. "Just who do you think you are?"

"Hello, Kevin." She tried for her best teacher voice, one she'd recently learned.

"If you think I've been hitting my kids, you should have come to me first. I would have told you to go to hell." His breath reeked of alcohol.

Looking around, she realized they were alone in the almost empty parking lot.

"Now you have Brenda and I trying to explain everything to the law. You know how Robert is; he thinks he owns the damn town." He leaned closer and she tried to hold her breath through the stench.

"I think this is a matter you'd be better off talking to CPS about." She took a step back and bumped into her car door. Her keys were in her hands and for a second, she thought she could use them in case she had to protect herself. Kevin still had an athletic build, but now he had a beer gut on him as well. He was shorter than she was but outweighed her by about eighty pounds.

"You've always been a busybody. Now you've taken my wife and kids away," Upon her empty look, he continued. "Oh, you didn't know that Brenda left me last night. Because of you, she's claiming I abused her and the kids. The damn state's given her full custody of my kids and I'm left high and dry." He leaned forward as she cringed against her car door.

"Maybe that's just what you wanted. To get me all to yourself?" His eyes raked up and down her simple tan slacks and blue top. She kept trying to pull back as he continued. "I remember you in school. Yeah, that tight little body of yours." He ran his eyes down her again. "Still looks tight. Maybe I should have paid more attention to you instead." He leaned against the car door, his hands on either side of her. His breath hitting her face with full force.

"If you think I want anything to...."

"Oh, I know you'd like it, honey. If I remember right, you always did like the jocks. I bet I could make you scream." He leaned back a little as he heard a car approaching. The car turned and started coming their way.

"I will make you scream." With these words he stormed off, got in his truck, and peeled out of the parking lot, leaving Allison leaning against her door, shaking.

When she did get in her car several minutes later, she sat there with the doors locked and her head against the steering wheel. Then when she started to drive, she ended up in the Golden Oar's parking lot instead of in front of her house. Walking in before she could change her mind, she headed for the bar area.

Sitting at the bar, she ordered herself a vodka cranberry and waited for the waiter to tell Iian she was there. Sure enough, not two minutes after her drink was set in front of her, he came strolling across the room with one of his sexy smiles on. Did he practice smiling in front of the mirror? Or did it just come naturally?

All she could think was, he sure knew how to walk. His long legs ate up the ground. He'd gotten a haircut since the last time she'd seen him. It was still longer than most men, but just above his collar now. She'd always been jealous of the thick black curly mass. She'd always wanted to run her hands through it, enjoying the feel. His white shirt and black pants looked neat and clean and she wondered how he could cook all day and still look fresh.

He came to a stop in front of her.

"Hello," he said and signed along.

"Hi, I'm just having a drink after a stressful day." She held up and shook her almost empty glass.

"What's wrong? The kids giving you trouble?" he signed while taking the seat next to hers.

"No, the parents." she left it short and vague. Knowing the news would have been all over the small town by now. She didn't think she wanted to be the one to spread the fact that it was because of her that a man's children and wife had been taken away from him.

Smiling over at him, and said, "How's your day going?" She sipped the last of her drink. "How's your sister? I've been meaning to stop by and tell her thanks for the cinnamon rolls she dropped off the other morning."

"Lacey's huge," he smiled, "and annoying. She keeps

77

trying to show up for work. I keep sending her home. I have to tell her it's doctor's orders," he shifted his weight on the seat.

Just then one of the wait staff came over and informed him he was needed in the back room.

"Give me just a moment," he signed.

"Sure, I've got time."

"Do you want another drink?" the bartender asked.

Allison looked at the thin balding man behind the counter and decided why not. She ordered another drink and crossed her legs and watched the room full of people.

Looking around, she studied the art and thought of her own art career. She enjoyed her first year in California. It had been hard work and she'd thrived with the attention it had brought her.

People came from all over the world to see it, some even plunking down thousands of dollars to own it. Then she'd had an art show in New York and everything had changed. She was no longer a small, no-named artist from smalls-ville Oregon.

She was Allison Adams, the next big "it" in the art world. Her pieces started selling for hundreds of thousands and it seemed she was in such high demand, she couldn't focus on where her art came from anymore. It was like her well had dried up. At the end of her second year in California, she'd only thought of one thing. Coming home.

Ric had persuaded her to apply for an art school in Paris. She'd always wanted to go to Paris, but to study under some of the best names in the art world was a different matter.

She didn't think that any amount of study would bring the passion back into her art. Looking around the room at the art that hung on the walls of the family restaurant, she felt a twinge in her chest. Her creative mind was starting to whirl back to life. She could feel it like the blood rushing from your head when you stood up too fast.

Setting down her almost-full glass, she tossed down some cash and started to leave.

Iian reached her just before she reached the front doors.

"Going so soon?" he asked.

"Yes, I've got to check on my mother. Thanks for the talk." She kissed his cheek and walked out, leaving him questioning what was going on with her.

When she drove up and parked in front of the house, she had a half dozen thoughts in her head about what she would paint. Never had the desire to paint been so strong before. She likened it to roaming a desert for years and suddenly stumbling upon an ocean.

She took the front porch stairs two at a time and came to a dead stop in front of the door.

There, sitting on her mother's beloved "Welcome" mat, sat what could only be described as a skinned animal. She'd been raised with cats that always liked to deliver their dead prey for show-and-tell. This animal didn't look like something had gotten to it. It looked like someone had done this.

She could see her mother on the other side of the large glass windows. She was vacuuming the living room while singing a song in a loud, off-key voice.

Whoever had left the poor skinned animal there, had meant it for her to see. Her mind raced to Kevin. Would he have done something like this to scare her?

Turning around, she looked up and down the quiet

street. She didn't see or hear anyone. There were no other cars parked along the road that didn't belong there. Setting her purse and bag down, she went around to the side of the house where they kept their trash can. She took the lid off, scooped up the carcass with her mother's favorite mat, and placed them inside the trash can. Then she took the can to the curb, thankful that tomorrow was trash collection day.

After heading inside, she realized that her desire to paint had faded.

Since school, Iian had been playing basketball with a group of friends at the Boys and Girls Club twice a week. He liked the physical activity. But today he needed it to get his mind off Allison and what he wanted to do to her.

When he'd first learned she was going to teach middle school art, he'd had a new fantasy involving her, where he sat in a small desk with her at the chalkboard. She wore a small, tight skirt, a button up white top that was too tight. The buttons were ready to burst over her chest. Her hair had been up in a loose bun. His mind continued on that thought until he was pushed by someone and almost landed on his butt.

As he was getting his ass handed to him by his friends, he wondered why he continued to show up every week. He was sore from working on the house and from sleeping on a couch that was a foot too small for his six-and-a-half-foot frame. But as he was fouled for the hundredth time by one of his best friends who didn't understand the term *"friendly game"*, he thought he was going crazy. He had bruises in places he didn't care to ice later. Of course, he knew how to play against his friends. He played the same way they did: fouling whenever he could. He was hot, sweaty, bruised and, to top it all off, he still couldn't get Ally out of his mind.

Aaron had joined the game several years back before he and Lacey had been married. Deciding he was a good match, they had quickly teamed up and been deemed the "dynamic duo" by everyone else.

He was just about to take a pass from his brother-in-law when he felt that familiar tingle on the back of his neck. It was more out of reflex that his head turned towards her. He remembers seeing her standing by the opened doors in a white, flowing sundress, then everything went white. Later he would try to convince himself that it was the ball hitting his head at one hundred miles per hour and not the way the sun had shone through her white skirt so that he could make out the outline of her long thin legs. He could have sworn the sun beamed around her golden hair and when it glowed, he heard angels singing. But he wasn't a pussy and didn't think things like that. Plus, he was deaf, so he couldn't have heard if there had been angels singing or not.

No, he thought as he laid on the hard gym floor, it was just the pass to the temple that had his head spinning.

"Oh, no! Are you alright?" She was bending over him, her cheeks pink and her blue eyes full of concern.

Aaron, the doctor in the room, stood back and laughed at his brother-in-law. First, there had been a concern. After all, it was a head injury that had caused Iian so much pain in his life. But seeing the man sprawled on the floor, bare-chested and ogling the concerned woman who all but had his head in her lap, he stepped back, along with the rest of his buddies. After all, Iian's scans and tests had come back clean. His brother-in-law was in perfect health.

"Aaron Stevens, you should know better than to throw a ball that hard at someone's head. How long have you been playing the sport anyway? And you call yourself a doctor!" She turned back to Iian, who hadn't tried to move off the floor.

Why would he want to move? Allison was bent over him; his head was damn near in her lap. He was as close as he'd ever gotten to her perfect breasts. He could even see them rise and fall when she talked to someone, he presumed Aaron, by the look of his brother-in-law's guilty face. Then she turned her attention back to him and he had to quickly move his eyes up from her silky white mounds to her rosy lips.

She smelled as good as she looked. Damn! Now he needed a cold shower.

She said something to him, but to be honest, he was so focused on when her tongue had darted out and licked those perfect lips, he hadn't paid attention.

"I'm sorry, can you repeat that? I couldn't quite tell what the three of you were saying," he said with a smile. He meant it to be a joke, but she pushed him into a sitting position and signed, "That's it, I'm driving you home. And before you argue with me, I saw your motorcycle out there. If you think I'm going to let you ride that death trap home with a head bump like that, you had better think again."

He wasn't going to argue. Actually, he wasn't even going to point out that Aaron, who was standing five feet away laughing, lived just down the road from him. A nice, slow drive home with Allison sounded just right.

"See you tomorrow," Aaron signed to him. He could tell he'd wanted to say more, but the look Allison gave him made him turn around and quickly walk away with the rest of the guys. He was positive they were all laughing at him. He didn't care, as long as there was a possibility of seeing her stand in the sunlight again.

"Whatever happened to playing basketball by the rules?" she signed after she helped him stand up. "The way you were playing out there, you're going to kill someone."

"Were you there long?" Iian signed to her. He was getting used to her knowing sign language and enjoyed being able to add her to the mix of people he could converse with.

"Yes," she said, but then she signed "no". She had a look in her eyes that matched the pink flush in her cheeks. She was guilty of something.

He looked down at his sweaty bare chest and teased her. "Oh, I see. You just wanted to see a bunch of grown man with their shirts off?"

"No." She blinked a few times, but he noticed her eyes went back to his chest quickly. "I had a meeting with Mr. Andrews, the director of the Boys and Girls Club. Then I heard the game and wandered down this way." She quickly started walking towards the double doors that led outside.

Catching up with her he signed, "Hang on a minute, let me grab my bag and shirt," as he pointed towards the bleachers. "You are going to take me home still?"

"Oh, yes, of course," she signed and waited as he walked across the court and retrieved his things.

She breathed a sigh of longing as he slipped on his shirt. It was such a shame to cover such a perfect chest and arms. Of the four men who were shirtless on the court, it was his chest that had been the one her eyes zeroed in on. Zeroed and remained on until he had been knocked silly by his brother-in-law.

Reverting her eyes to his face, she tried to give him a casual smile.

Had she really agreed to drive him home? What was she thinking? She wasn't thinking. How could she think when he had looked up at her with those silvery eyes? The rest of his face didn't help focus her mind either. His nose was straight with a tiny jump at the end. She wanted to run her fingers down the fun slope. His jaw was strong and firm, with the slightest cleft in his chin. She wanted to play her tongue just there. All in all, Iian Jordan was a very nice package. She knew how big of a player he was in the past and had avoided anything more than just a friendship with him. She didn't even know what he really thought of her. Maybe he saw her as a sister? He'd kissed her a few times and the last few kisses had given her cause to think that he wasn't thinking of her in a sisterly way. She was still trying to figure him out on the drive to his house.

Lacey and Todd had always treated her and Abby like their little sisters, especially since Lacey had spent three years babysitting the two of them. She remembers Iian having to tag along several times when his dad and Todd had been overseas on a trip.

As they drove to his house in a silent car with him sitting next to her, she kept trying to sneak peaks out of the corner of her eyes. He had an even better side profile.

Iian enjoyed the drive home. Since he wasn't driving, he spent most of the time looking at Allison. In the gym, he saw something in her eyes. He was sure when he'd first looked at her it was concern, but then it had quickly turned to something more. He thought it might have been arousal.

One of the very first things he noticed about her back in the first grade was her hair. Back then it had been a lot longer. Her mother had always kept Abby's and Allison's hair long when they were younger. Somewhere in middle school, the girls had gained some freedom, and both had chopped their hair short. Iian remembers feeling depressed the whole month after Ally had cut hers to just above her shoulders.

In junior high, she had let it grow out again and it reached to the middle of her back. Now it was just below her shoulders and he thought the style suited her best. Most of the time when he saw her, she had it up in a braid or a ponytail. Today she wore it down and a little curly. He liked it best when it had a little curl to it. He thought it would be just as soft as it looked. His hands itched to reach across the seat and touch it, but he kept them tucked by his side instead.

Finally, they reached his place. The house sat like a beacon in the night. Every light had been left on downstairs.

"Having a party?" she signed after stopping her car in front of his door and shutting the engine off.

"No. I guess the carpet guys left all the lights on. They had to finish a few things after installing my new carpet the other day."

"Oh, you got new carpet?" She asked.

"Just upstairs in all the bedrooms. I've just remodeled them. Would you like to come in and see?" he asked, hoping she would. Anything to get to stay in her company longer.

"No, I'd better get back to my mom. I don't like to leave her for long. Mrs. Evans keeps an eye on her, but I've been gone almost three hours." She chewed her bottom lip.

"What was the meeting with Bob about?" he asked, deciding to change the subject off from her mother and the stress it was obviously causing her.

"Who?" she asked, trying to take her eyes off his hands as he signed. He had large strong hands.

"Bob Andrews, the director of the Boys and Girls Club. You did say you had a meeting with him, right?"

"Oh, yes. Well, I've been teaching an art class at school and I was looking into renting one of the classrooms, so I could add a summer program there."

"You're going to teach at the Boys and Girls Club?" He sat up a little straighter.

"I'm thinking about it." She looked at him and he could tell that he had the funniest look on his face. "Okay, tell me what gives. What's that face for?"

How could he tell her he was having one of those fantasies about her in a tight black skirt, a sheer white top with the buttons lose, her hair up in a bun and sexy teacher glasses on. Damn! He really needed that cold shower.

"I. I..." could he really stutter using sign language? "I think it's great! I think the kids would enjoy having you as a teacher for the summer."

"Really? I've enjoyed teaching so far. I think a summer class would be fun."

"What about your art? Your career?"

"No matter where I am, what I'm doing, I will always paint and draw. To be honest," she turned her whole body and faced him, "I'd sort of lost my desire to paint in California. Then just last week, I started to paint again. I took up the brush and wonderful things came to me. I'm glad I'm out of California. Oh, I enjoyed it for a while. But I started missing the relaxation of being home. Now that my mom requires so much of my time, I don't think I could ever leave again."

He saw the sadness in her eyes. "You know you have a whole town that's not only able but willing, to watch out for your mother."

"Oh, I don't look at her as a burden. It's just I thought I would have made it to Paris once in my life. Before I left California, I actually put in an application to attend school there." She was starting to feel down and lost.

"Paris?" He had never been, but both his brother and sister had been there. Actually, Todd and Megan owned a small chateau just outside of the city. Megan had inherited it after her brother Matt had passed away.

She smiled over at him and continued. "You must think I'm some silly schoolgirl talking about my dreams."

"Schoolgirl? I thought I was talking to the new art teacher?" He smiled at her.

"Yes, yes, you are. Thank you, Iian. Talking to you has helped me." She leaned over and aimed for placing a casual kiss on his cheek. She had misjudged, and the kiss ended up half on his cheek and half on his lips.

He tensed, then pulled her into his arms and his mouth was on hers.

Not only was this the longest conversation he's had with a woman who wasn't his sister, in ten years, it was a conversation he was whole-heartily involved in. He really cared what she wanted in life. He had gone years without knowing she could paint and draw like she did. He was getting to know more and more about her dreams and wishes and he wanted to keep learning.

Taking his time with the kiss, he decided it was time he showed her that he was interested in her. And the best way of doing that was pulling her into his lap, right there in her car in front of his house.

She tasted like strawberries. Okay! He knew how cliché that sounded, but she did. Pulling back, he looked into her unfocused eyes.

"Strawberries?"

"Mmm." She ran her tongue over her lips and shook her head and smiled. "Lip gloss."

Pulling his head back to hers, he took the kiss deeper.

She reached under his shirt and played her fingers over his muscles, running her mouth down his neck.

He fought to stay in control. Hell! He'd gotten so hard when he'd pulled her onto his lap, his eyes had teared up. As she played her long fingers over his damp skin, he was minutes away from dragging her in the back seat of her car and taking her right there.

Then she pulled back quickly.

"I'm sorry," she said and pulled her phone out of her purse. "My phone." She held it up, so he could see that it was ringing.

When she answered it, her whole attitude changed.

He read her lips. "What! She's at your store naked?"

Less than ten minutes later, Allison walked her mother into their house wrapped in one of Patty O'Neil's extra blankets from the store. Her mother had apparently shown up there at half-past eight that evening. Her purse in hand, she had grabbed a shopping cart and proceeded to do her shopping, stark naked.

Allison thought that if the situation wasn't so dire, she would have had a good laugh.

CHAPTER 7

a few days later, it was one of those evenings where she was glad she was home. Teaching younger kids art sure had its ups and downs, but for the most part, she was enjoying her new job.

Her mom was just finishing the dishes in the kitchen, something she said she didn't want help with tonight. Allison had taken a glass of wine out to the front porch and was sitting in a small rocker watching the sun start to slide down over the water. It was cool out; she had her light blue jacket on to keep the warmth in. Her feet were tucked up underneath her and she was enjoying the quiet.

Her mother hadn't had any more "episodes" since the other evening. How was she supposed to watch her all the time? Mrs. Evans was keeping an eye out and several of the church women stopped by the house regularly during the day. The fact was, no one could watch her every moment of every day.

Allison had actually completed one of her new pieces for a charity she'd been thinking of donating to. She was excited about the few pieces she was doing for them and felt an inner peace about the project.

She heard a loud rumble and turned to watch a figure on a motorcycle coming from down the street. She knew it was Iian before he was close enough to see. He was driving slowly, and she could see he was wearing light-colored jeans with a dark gray zip-up jacket. His sunglasses shaded his eyes from her and she realized he hadn't seen her at first. He passed her house, but then slowed down and did a big loop in her neighbor's driveway and returned to stop in front of her yard. He sat for a while, letting the machine run for a minute.

Smiling to her, he signed, "Want to go for a ride?"

It was either the smile or the casual way he sat on the large machine that made him look irresistible. Deciding to take a chance, she signed back, "Sure, hang on and let me tell my mom," which made her feel like a teenager.

Sitting out front of her place, he was glad he had decided to ride the bike today. Not only did he enjoy riding it, but it gave him a chance to be with her. Smiling as she came bouncing down her walk, he thought of how she would feel behind him, pressed up against his back.

He watched her stop a foot from his bike and stare at it. It was an old Harley he'd bought on his twenty-first birthday. It had taken him eleven months and almost a year's salary to get it purring underneath him like it was currently doing. The matte black finish had cost him, but it accented the seat and pipes so well. The seat had been a special present from his sister; the ostrich leather had been exactly what he'd wanted. No doubt his sister had snuck onto his computer and noticed he'd been eying it.

Now Allison just stood and looked at it and he didn't think she was taking in the seat or the paint job.

She was looking as if she was trying to figure out how to get on it.

Bending down, he flipped the back-foot pegs and motioned for her to get on.

Placing her hand lightly on his shoulder, she tried as smoothly as she could to hoist her leg over the back and sit down. It took some doing, but finally, she sat squarely on the seat and had each foot on the pegs.

"You'll want to lean forward and hold onto me," he said over his shoulder. "When I turn, lean with me."

When she leaned forward and lightly took hold of his jacket sides, he chuckled to himself. He could fix that.

Pushing up, he kicked up his kick-stand. He would just have to get her to hold onto him tighter. Smiling to himself, he took off. By the end of the street, she was right where he'd wanted her to be. Her front was tight against his back, her arms had reached around and were holding on tightly around his waist. He could feel her excitement as he hit the outskirts of town.

She had never ridden on a motorcycle before. It was louder than she imagined and the vibrations under her were soothing. As Iian drove fast, she enjoyed the wind and speed. But what she really enjoyed was holding onto him. His shoulders were wide, protecting her from the strongest winds of the speed. Her arms had skirted around his waist after the first few blocks when she realized she would need a better hold on him if she wanted to stay on the bike. She could feel his muscles in his stomach and wondered how he had gotten such a nice six-pack. Then she wondered what the rest of him looked like.

Resting her head on his shoulder, she enjoyed the beautiful drive. He had taken one of the best scenic routes, one that she knew would end up at an overlook close to the state park. where a lot of teenagers liked to go to make out. She had even gone there a few times in high school. Smiling into his back, she vibrated with anticipation.

Pulling the bike to a stop in a small but secluded area of the park, he looked out over the water and remembered why he lived in the Northwest. Not only was tonight a great night to be on a ride, but he had timed it just right. The sun was in the process of setting and the whole sky was a rainbow of colors, which reflected off the low layer of clouds that hung just over the water.

Switching off the bike, he pushed down the kick-stand. Turning to Allison he saw the wonder in her eyes.

"Did you miss this in the city?" he asked.

Never taking her eyes off the horizon, she just nodded.

Taking her hand, he waited until she dismounted from the bike. Then he swung his leg and easily dismounted as well. She had watched him, but when he noticed, she blushed slightly and walked towards the rock fence that lined the edge of the walkway.

Coming to stand behind her, he pulled her back into

him. Holding her tight as the sun slid slowly beyond their sight.

She let out a sigh and turned to him. "That was the most beautiful sunset I've seen in years. Thank you."

He smiled and then leaned down to claim her mouth. It seemed like all he had thought about since kissing her last was reclaiming her lips. Her arms reached up and around his shoulders. One of her hands went into his hair, holding him close.

He enjoyed holding her. She was taller than most women and she seemed to fit his tall frame perfectly. Her head was just half a foot lower, which made it perfect for him to kiss her and run his mouth down that hot neck of hers. Her taste was sweet and hinted at something forbidden. Her hands were holding him to her and he didn't mind how tight she was gripping onto his hair.

When he slowly pushed her jacket open, he thought he would burst into flames seeing the tight white tee-shirt that was all but see through. Pulling it up and away, he enjoyed exploring the soft skin that he had exposed. Allison had always been athletic but seeing the softness of her hip and stomach did something to him. He was sure he was moaning like a teenager when he pulled her top up to expose the simple white lace that held two of the most perfect mounds he'd ever had the pleasure of seeing.

Looking up into her face he could see the pleasure there. Her eyes were slits as she watched him through her lashes. A small smile formed on her lips and her tongue darted out to lick her bottom lip, swollen from his kisses.

Bending his head, he ran his lips gently over the lace, wetting it until he felt her nipples peak against his tongue. Then he pushed it aside until he could enjoy the silky pink nub. Her back arched, exposing more of her skin to his torture. His eyes darted to her face again. He could see that her head had fallen back, and her hands were gripping the rock wall behind her. He wanted to see her face, he wanted to see her eyes, so he could know what she was feeling, what he was doing to her.

Would she moan or scream when he pushed her to the breaking point? Running his hands down her side, he continued on the path to the snap of her jeans. As he ran his tongue around her taunt peaks, he used his hands to lightly pull at the material until he had exposed another barrier of simple white lace. The snap of her jeans was easy to pull open as she shifted her feet wider. Watching her face, he ran his fingers lightly under the lace. Her eyes were dark, and she nibbled on her bottom lip in anticipation.

"What do you want Ally?" he teased as his fingers started to run slightly below the material. He saw her take in a breath, then her head rolled back again, and he turned his attention to the softness he had just exposed.

Her skin was hot and felt so good. Her pant legs tied her up, but he knew that if she could she would have flung her legs wider. Her hands had come to his hair once more, holding him to her breast as he played his fingers over her, then slipped inside slowly and he was sure he moaned out loud. He lapped her up until he felt her core vibrating in his hands, then enjoyed feeling her convulsing around him. Had he thought she'd tasted sweet before? He was sure there had been nothing more perfect than having her, but now everything changed after she had come for him.

Still kissing her he started to pull her pants back in place when he felt her tense. Looking over his shoulder, he saw the lights of a car coming up the long-secluded drive. He turned to protect her from the high beams.

～

"Well, well, what do we have here?" Kevin Williams said as he slammed his truck door. Allison could hear the slur in his words and knew that he was drunk.

Iian stood in front of her, his large shoulders shielding her from Kevin's view, so she quickly zipped her jacket and buttoned her pants. Not caring if everything was in place, she started to pull on Iian's hand, trying to get him to get back on the bike and get out of there quickly.

"Slutting around with a Jordan are we Allison?"

She knew Iian couldn't have read his lips since he was standing to the side of the bright headlights blinding them.

The tension in Allison's hands said more than the words Kevin had spoken. It took only a moment for Iian's eyes to adjust to the light hitting him full force.

"Having another *free* night are you, Kevin?" Iian said. He planted his feet wide as Allison continued to pull on his arm.

"Shut up!" Kevin started to walk forward.

"Do you really want to do this now?" Iian asked calmly. Kevin stopped his forward motion.

Taking another look at Iian, he tossed the beer bottle he'd emptied over the cliff.

"Can't even come up here for a beer anymore," he mumbled. Turning back to his truck, he waited until he was hidden behind the bright lights to say, "You'll regret this, you bitch... choosing him over me. I swear you'll regret this."

She felt Iian vibrate, but still held his hand and quickly pulled him backward. She didn't know if he had read Kevin's lips but doubted it since she couldn't even see his outline in the bright lights.

When his truck had disappeared down the road, she released a large breath.

"I'm sorry about that," Iian said to her. "He's had a thing out for me since middle school." He was looking at her with such kindness, she didn't want to tell him the whole story.

Shaking her head, she tried to smile at him. "I'd better get back home."

Iian took his time going down the hill and she enjoyed the feel of him as she plastered herself against his back.

When they drove back up to the front of her house, she was just getting off the motorcycle when she heard the back door of her house slam shut. Jumping a little, she looked towards the back of the house in time to see a large, dark figure running away.

Iian was off the bike and besides her, wondering what had caused the troubled look. Looking to where she had, he saw nothing.

"What's wrong?" He asked.

"I thought I saw someone leaving out the back door," she signed. He turned and looked again. This time, she felt his whole-body tense beside her.

"Stay here," he said and signed at the same time. Rushing towards the house, Allison saw then what she hadn't before.

A slight glow was coming from the living room windows. She could see smoke coming from the kitchen window and smelled a distinct smell of something burning.

"Mom? Mom?" She ran towards the place screaming, only to be yanked back by strong hands.

"Don't!" Iian screamed.

"My mom!" She turned back and signed to him.

Turning back around, Allison started to race towards the house again, only to be pulled up short once again by Iian.

"Iian! She's in there! My Mom is in there!"

"Make the call." He pushed his cell phone into her hands.

Removing his jacket, he rushed to the neighbor's side-yard and dunked the light material in a bucket of water which sat in-between the houses. Looking back, he saw Ally standing and staring at the house as she talked into his phone.

Hopping the fence between the houses, he raced towards the back door. The glass was shattered, and smoke was pouring out. He couldn't see any flames, just smoke. Pulling the door wide, he stood back as the smoke billowed out. Pulling the wet jacket over his head, he took a deep breath and raced into the dark room.

Where was her mother? Where was Iian? She had watched him race towards the back of the house. Had it been five minutes ago? Was it just two seconds ago? Worry had time standing still. Thinking of her mother, she started to walk closer to the house that was engulfed in flames.

"Mom!" she screamed. Just then the living room window blew out and rained glass over her head. Covering her face and ears, she watched as her living room curtains caught fire.

"No! Mom! Iian!" At this point, two of her neighbors had come out to see what all the shouting was about. Mrs. Evans rushed over to where she stood.

"Have you seen my mother?" she screamed.

"No, dear. I thought she was with you. Oh, dear, I hope she isn't in that."

Rushing forward, she ignored the warnings from her neighbors. Reaching the front door, she grabbed the door handle, her hand burning on the hot metal. Pulling it back, she removed her jacket and using it, tried the handle again. Pulling the door open, she ducked down as a plume of smoke poured out.

Screaming for her mother, she inched towards the door only to come up short against a small mound just inside the doorway. Grabbing a handful of her mother's shirt, she yanked and pulled her to safety.

When she reached the end of the porch, Steve, another neighbor, lifted her mother up and carried her to safety. Seeing her neighbors surround her mother, she raced around the back of the house to find Iian.

The back door stood open and smoke was flowing from the dark hole. Knowing he couldn't hear her, she raced into the burning house without a second thought. After all, he had rushed in after her mother. How could she let him be consumed by the fire?

Ducking down, she was only a few feet in when she felt his hand grab her. He yanked her off her feet, carting her over his shoulders as he marched back out the door.

"Damn it, Ally! I told you to stay put!" he said and then coughed a few times as he pulled her away from the heat. Looking at him, she saw that his clothes were steaming from being in the house too long.

"I've got my mother. She's out." She tried to sign, but her hand was hurting like crazy from where she had grabbed the door handle, so she had to speak instead of use sign language.

He reached to take her hand and pull her towards the front of the building but came up short when she flinched away and held her hand close to her chest. Pulling her hand down to look at it, he saw deep red marks crossing her palm.

"You're hurt!" He grabbed her arm and walked her to the front of the building. By now she could hear the fire trucks just down the street. When they came around the cornered the building, she could see her mother was sitting on Mrs. Evans' front porch with blankets around her shoulders. Pulling free from Iian, she rushed over to her.

"Mom!" She knelt beside her mother and took her hand. "Mom, are you alright?"

Her mother was coughing and had a glass of water in her hand. Allison saw that her hair was singed, and her clothes were streaked black. Her mother's eyes were red and she was blinking continuously, trying to clear them.

"Here, drink some more." She helped her mother drink the water. Her hands were shaking, and she felt like she couldn't get her breath. She couldn't bear to turn around and see what was going on behind her with the house.

Iian was beside her then. He saw the flashing lights of the fire trucks and looked back over at the house. It was a complete loss.

CHAPTER 8

*A*llison was sitting in the waiting room at Edgeview, again, with her burned hand close to her body to protect it. It had been cleaned, medicated, and wrapped up tight. Iian hadn't left her side once since they'd arrived at the hospital. They were waiting on word from the doctor-on-staff about her mother's condition. She'd ridden in the ambulance with her, talking to her the entire way. Her mother hadn't said anything, just coughed and blinked her eyes.

When they had driven up, Iian's motorcycle was parked by the doors, and he stood there holding his phone. He must have texted his sister and brother-in-law because they had shown up within fifteen minutes. Aaron, dressed in a dark dinner jacket, had immediately gone to check on her mother.

Lacey was wearing a long flowing purple dress that was tight around her seven-months-pregnant belly. She quickly crossed the room, sat down next to her, and pulled her into a light hug. Then she noticed her burned hand and reached for it. Looking over the bandages, Allison noticed tears in her friend's eyes.

"I'm so sorry about your house. How bad is your hand? How is your mother?"

"My hand is fine, just slightly second-degree burning on my palm. My mother..." She paused and looked over at Iian, who was pacing the waiting room floor. His sister looked over at him and signed for him to sit down. He looked at Lacey and then looked at Allison and quickly walked over and sat next to her, pulling Allison's good hand into his own.

Lacey smiled upon seeing the gesture.

"They haven't told us anything about my mom yet. I rode in the ambulance with her, she was awake for the ride. I didn't see any burns on her." She took a deep breath and closed her eyes. "Her hair was singed, and her clothes were covered in soot. She was lying by the front door. Why was she just lying there? When I found her she, was out. Maybe she passed out?" She felt something clawing at her insides, "Maybe she fell and hit her head?" She knew she was babbling but didn't care. What if she'd gotten there a few minutes later? What if she hadn't found her? A million scenarios started to play in her head.

Then she felt Iian's hand tighten on hers and looked up at him.

Lacey jumped in. "Ally, you were there on time, you found her. She's going to be alright. See, here's Aaron." They stood and watched Aaron walk across the room, his dinner jacket had been replaced with a white doctor's coat.

"First off, let me assure you that your mother is fine. We're moving her to a private room. She was very lucky, and she has no burns. She does have a large gash on the back of her head, some bruises, and of course, smoke inhalation. We've got her on oxygen and have given her a local and some stitches for her wound." He'd been signing all the while for Iian's sake. When he stopped, he pulled his wife close to his side. "Come on, I'll take you up to her room."

Just as they were leaving the waiting room, Megan rushed into the lobby holding little Matthew's hand; Todd was beside her holding their sleeping daughter.

Megan rushed over and hugged Allison. "How is she?"

"We're just going to see her now. Can they come along?" Allison asked Aaron.

"I don't see why not." Everyone followed Aaron into the elevator, where Matthew quickly asked if he could push the button.

Aaron bent down and looked him directly in the face and said, "If you can find the number four, you can push that button for us."

Matthew's little face squished up as he looked at the numbered buttons. It took a few seconds, but then his little fingers hovered over the number four. Looking to his mother and getting a nod of encouragement, he pushed the button and they were on their way.

When they walked into the room, Allison noticed a few things. Her mother's hair was standing up on end and the nurses were trying to draw blood. Her mother was fighting them and Allison rushed over to help. The oxygen mask had slipped up to cover one of her mother's eyes. Aaron was by her side, helping hold her mother's hands down.

"Mom, calm down. They just need to draw some blood. Hold still for the doctor." Her mother was losing strength.

Allison saw it then; a large bruise that ran over her mother's bicep. Holding her mother's hand, she looked over at Aaron. He'd seen it, too.

"Allison?" Her mother blinked up at her several times and relaxed back onto the bed.

"Yes, Mom, I'm here. Doctor Stevens is just going to draw some blood." Aaron walked over and took the needle from the nurse who looked like she'd been through a tornado. As she stepped aside to let him draw the blood, she righted her clothing and hair.

"I've had healthy children fight me with that much strength. I think your mother is in fine enough health." She smiled as she took the vials from Aaron that were full of blood.

After getting the blood, Aaron said, "Mrs. Adams, I just want to check your arms and neck area, if that's okay with you."

Her mother sat still, and since her oxygen mask was in place again, nodded in agreement.

Allison was by his side, she saw the bruises and she especially saw when he mimicked how a man's hand had placed them on her mother's bicep.

"Very good. We're going to let you get some rest. You just hit the button here," he placed the call button pad by her hand, "if you need anything."

Stepping back, Allison followed him into the hallway, where it appeared everyone else had settled while Allison and Aaron been fighting to draw blood.

"Allison," Aaron started to say.

"Who did that to her?" Allison's fists were clenched. "Those are bruises from a man's hands."

"I was just going to ask if there was someone else at the house tonight?"

She felt the world tilt. "I saw a man leaving," she whispered. Iian was by her side then. "Oh my God. The cut on her head?"

"We'll look into it. Now that I think there might be foul play, I'll have to call the police."

At one o'clock in the morning, Allison and the police had more questions than answers.

Her mother had been attacked. Hit over the head with one of her beloved crystal candlesticks most likely, and the fire had been started on purpose. The large can of gasoline had quickly been spotted in the kitchen area, or what used to be her kitchen. Her mother's arms and back had been photographed, and the police were going to investigate to find out more.

Her mother's eyes were red and swollen shut for the most part. Allison sat by her side all evening, only leaving the room to talk with the police or Aaron. Iian sat quietly in the corner of the room. When the room would quiet down, they would talk using sign language to talk to each other as her mother slept. She was grateful to have him stay. Last time she'd spent an all-nighter in one of these rooms, she'd had a miserable time by herself.

They talked about the town, about her art, about her stay in California. Then she'd asked questions about the restaurant, about cooking, and anything else that popped into her head. He was doing a great job of taking her mind off the fact that all she had left in the world was her mother and the clothes on her back.

She dreaded going through town and seeing the shell

of what used to be her family home, knowing everything was gone. She tried hard to focus on what she had left.

By the next morning, Allison was longing for a hot shower. Her hair and clothing smelled of smoke. Her eyes were burning, dry, and itchy. She'd gotten about two hours of sleep but desperately wished for more.

Iian walked back into the room with two full plates of breakfast from the cafeteria. What she wanted the most was the large cup of coffee he'd balanced on top of the Styrofoam containers. Her mother had been in and out of sleep most of the night. Currently, she was sitting up in the hospital bed enjoying a hot breakfast. She was watching the news and ate her food like she had no cares in the world.

"It's so nice to get away every now and then" her mother had told her when the staff had delivered her breakfast. She wished she could look at life with such wonderment herself.

Less than an hour after breakfast, Megan and Lacey walked in with two large bouquets of flowers. Several more vases of flowers had been delivered earlier that morning. The room was quickly filling up and smelled like a flower garden.

Lacey sat next to her mother, talking quietly to her while Megan sat on the couch next to Iian. Iian hadn't left, and she was sure he smelled as bad as she did. Yet he looked fresh as if he'd just arrived there after a great night's sleep and a hot shower.

"So, I've decided. You're moving in." Megan held up a bright red key chain. The silver key dangling on it caught the light.

"What?" She didn't think her mind was that tired, but

she wasn't quite understanding what Megan was talking about.

"I've given you the honeymoon suite. It's yours indefinitely." Then it hit her. Megan's cabins. She had five of them that she rented out for her bed and breakfast business.

Allison had done paintings of all the cabins and the main house several years ago for her. The honeymoon suite, which Megan called it, was the largest cabin with two rooms, a large bathroom, its own kitchen and living room area. And the cabin was just a quick walk from the beach.

"I couldn't possibly," she got no further than that.

"You wouldn't dare turn this away. Not after everything you've done for me." Allison could see tears starting to form in her friend's eyes. "I won't take no for an answer." She put the key into her hands.

"I've brought you a change of clothes. If you want, why don't you go to the bathroom there and shower and change? It can't be comfortable sitting around in the same smoky clothes all night," Lacey said, as she sat by Mrs. Adams' side.

Looking between the two, Allison wondered what she'd ever do without her friends.

"I... Thank you." Tears threatened the back of her eyes. Quickly standing up she took the large bag from Lacey and retreated into the privacy of the bathroom.

When she came out, her mother was asleep, and the room was empty except for Megan, who sat reading a book on the couch.

"Aaron and Lacey had some things to take care of. Todd has the children with him if you want to go home and get some rest. I'll stay here for a few hours with your mother. Mary is going to stop by in a few hours to take over. I think there is a list going around of everyone who has volunteered to sit with your mom. You needn't worry about her for the rest of the day."

"I can't thank you enough for letting me stay in your cabin. I hadn't thought that far ahead."

"Don't worry about it. That's what we do for family." Megan smiled over at her. "We've filled up the kitchen, so there's plenty of food. Go on, get some rest. Oh, I almost forgot," Megan reached into her purse and pulled out a set of keys. "We found them on the front porch last night, so we drove your car over this morning for you. It's parked in the West lot, right up front."

She'd been so good about holding everything inside, but when she reached her car it all came out. Resting her head on the steering wheel, she cried until she couldn't cry anymore.

CHAPTER 9

The drive through town was the hardest one she'd ever taken. When she'd reached her street, she tried to avoid looking down to see what was left of her childhood home. From the description the police officer had given last night, she knew there hadn't been much left.

Deciding it was too much for her to handle just now she quickly turned down a side road and headed towards the cabin.

Parking in the gravel driveway next to the sign that read, "Pride Bed and Breakfast" she realized she didn't even have her purse. It had been left in the house last night when she'd spontaneously taken her ride with Iian.

The path to the cabins was well traveled. Megan had done wonders with the plants along the short walk. Small signs poked out of the daisies that read, "Don't trample on the daisies – the fairies"

Several flower beds had bird feeders, bird baths,

gnomes, or other small statues along the pathway. All in all, it was an enjoyable walk past the other four cabins.

Standing in the sunlight, she stopped to look at her cabin, otherwise known as the honeymoon suite. She could tell why Megan had chosen this one for its purpose. Not only was it farthest away from the main house, but it was the most secluded cabin. The other cabins sat directly on the main path, while this cabin was off on its own little pathway and sat further back in the trees. The view from the large front porch was breathtaking. The ocean and beach filled her vision as far as she could see. With the woods to its back and the ocean at its front, she didn't have to wonder why people had come from across the world to stay here. And it was all hers, indefinitely.

Using the silver key to unlock the red door, she walked in to find the front living area full of flowers, boxes, and bags of items. Setting her keys down, she wandered around the room opening bags and boxes. There were shoes in her size and her mother's. Clothing of all types for both of them. Kitchen supplies, make-up, a blow dryer, curling irons, you name it, it was there in a bag or a box. Some of them were used items, but in good condition, but most of them were new. All with notes from the person or people who had given without a second thought. She read and collected each note as she went through the items. She thought she'd cried all she could in her car, but the tears gently seeped out, washing away all her loneliness.

Iian was in a mood. He'd left the hospital with his sister, only because she'd blackmailed him. Having a sister who knew and saw everything was sometimes a burden. He couldn't deny the fact that he'd needed a shower and a few hours of sleep himself. In fact, he caught himself falling asleep several times on the car trip home.

Knowing that Allison was getting rest had set his mind at ease, at least, for a few hours in order for him to get some much-needed rest.

Dumping his clothes in the dirty bin, he walked naked into his newly-renovated bathroom and stopped dead.

There, as clear as day, stood his father. Blinking his eyes several times to clear them, he was sure he was hallucinating. But what happened next shocked him to the core.

"Well, don't stand there butt-naked boy. Grab that towel and cover your shame," the old man said and then laughed loudly. All perfectly heard by a man who'd been dead for over ten years.

Iian hit the floor.

"Shit!" Todd said as he shook his naked and unconscious brother for what seemed like the hundredth time. It had been over eleven hours since his sister had dropped him off to get a shower and some rest. They'd been texting him for the last two hours until finally, he'd driven over himself to see what was keeping his brother from answering.

Walking into the main bathroom, the last thing he'd expected to see was his brother naked, lying on the cold tile floor. It had taken him almost a minute to rouse him.

Iian blinked a few times, then he focused on his brother's face. His brother was talking to him, but he couldn't hear.

Had he imagined the whole thing? Was he going crazy? He must have been more tired than he thought last night.

"I saw Dad," he signed to Todd. "He spoke to me and I could hear him."

"What the hell are you talking about? Are you okay?" Todd signed.

Standing up, he steadied himself by leaning on the countertop. He shook his head and turned towards his brother to tell him again.

Todd interrupted with, "Don't stand there butt-naked. Grab that towel and cover your shame."

Iian looked at his brother and just laughed.

Half an hour later, he sat in Megan and Todd's living room along with every person in town, waiting for Allison and her mother to arrive. Little Sara had crawled up in his lap shortly after arriving and had quickly fallen asleep, leaving him stuck sitting on the couch in one of the busiest rooms in the house and he didn't mind one bit.

People came and went, all chatting while waiting for the two people they'd come to show their support to. Not being able to hear sometimes had its perks.

He could tell when the pair arrived. The energy level in the place tripled. Everyone in the room quickly rushed towards the hallway. He sat there holding his niece and enjoying the warm feeling of a sleeping child on his chest.

Allison and her mother walked in the front door and were greeted by the whole town of Pride.

Less than ten minutes later, Lacey walked Allison into

the den with a plate full of food in her hands. She edged into the crowded room and saw Iian sitting on a large couch against the opposite wall. The sleeping baby on his shoulder was beautiful, but when he looked up from the little girl and smiled at her, she melted.

Walking over, she gently sat beside him, trying not to disturb the baby. Since his hands were full, he spoke softly and asked, "How's your hand?"

He was looking down at the newly re-bandaged hand. She could see the concern in his eyes. When he looked back up she said clearly, "It's fine. I didn't get a chance to say thank you for staying with me at the hospital."

When he just smiled, she bent over and started to eat a little off her plate. Several times, he reached over with his free hand and took a carrot or half her roll from her plate. It was nice, sitting in a packed room next to the one person she didn't feel like she had to hold a conversation with. Someone she suddenly felt closer to than anyone else in the room. When she started to rise to get some dessert, she looked over her shoulder and asked if he wanted something from the dessert table.

He gently shifted the baby on his shoulder and stood, then said, "I'll get something myself. Let me just take her upstairs for her nap."

"I'll go with you." She followed him up the large staircase and down the long hallway to the light pink room decorated with butterflies.

When he gently placed his niece on her pink comforter in her crib, he tucked the blanket loosely over her and pushed a strand of her blonde curls from her face. Reaching over, he turned on the baby monitor and grabbed the receiver. When he turned around he signed, "For her mother," and smiled again.

When he walked out the door, he pulled her into his arms and kissed her. It was a light kiss, but it warmed her to her toes. When it ended, he held on for just a moment. He needed to hold her, feel her in his arms and she needed it as well. Then they headed down to get dessert together, holding hands.

It was great to see everyone in town come together for someone in need. The gifts and donations she and her mother had received the previous day had been a blessing; one they hadn't even had the time to think but sitting in a room full of her town's people assured her one thing, she and her mother would never want for anything.

Patty, the owner of the town's only grocery store, was sitting next to her mother listening to her talk about all the wonderful things they'd been given as if it was Christmas.

Allison was sitting in the dining room talking to a group of people she'd gone to school with when Lacey approached her with a small package in her hands.

"I know you've been given a lot these last few days, but I thought you might need one more thing." She set the package down in front of her.

Allison started to remove the yellow flowered paper and looked down into her own face. The family portrait had been taken less than two months before her father had passed away from a heart attack. She and her sister stood on either side of her father as their mother sat in front. It had been the last family portrait taken of a family about to be torn apart.

Tears stung her eyes and her hand shook as she ran a finger lightly over her sister's face.

That's when it really had hit her. She'd lost everything in that fire. The years of family portraits, her great-grand-mother's piano, her grandfather's clock, all of her sister's belongings and memories.

Looking down at the framed picture, she realized this was the last thing she had to remind her of what was once a great family. Then she looked up into the faces of the town people who had come out to show their love and support and realized she still had a wonderful family.

Her mother, for the most part, had enjoyed the evening. Since the other night, she hadn't had another episode. Allison knew the reprieve would be short-lived.

Tanya was there with her kids. Her new boss had taken the time to assure her that she could take as much time as she needed to recover. Allison didn't want to take any time off. She knew she had to find someplace to put her mother. Getting back to work was going to help her keep her mind off the large black hole that was her old house.

She'd finally driven by it earlier on her way to pick up her mother from the hospital. The charred remains of her house loomed over the neighborhood. The east wall of the house still stood, but everything else had fallen in on itself. The foundation could be seen on the far-right side of the place. She could actually still smell smoke when she drove by. Someone had come by and placed a condemned sign up, trying to detour anyone from entering. Like anyone would want to try to step foot in a place that looked like it would blow over with a slight wind.

Just then from across the room, she heard the tone of

her mother's voice change and knew it was time to leave the party.

The next day Allison decided she did need help with her mother.

Living in an eight-hundred-square-foot cabin by yourself was one thing. Living with your mother who was in the full stages of dementia was another.

Several times she'd been woken from her sleep with the banging of pots. Did they even have pots? was her first thought. Then when she'd heard a loud crash, she'd jumped from her bed and ran in to find her mother on her hands and knees scrubbing the bathroom floor. Scrubbing it at two in the morning.

When she'd asked her what she was doing, her mother had replied.

"I'm cleaning up after your father. He just barfed all over the bathroom floor and I can't seem to get it up."

When Allison looked at the shiny linoleum, she quickly realized the issue. The tile in their house had been white, not tan.

CHAPTER 10

*J*ian loved working outside in the dirt. He enjoyed working in the yard as much as he liked cooking in his kitchens.

The weather had turned, so he could finally till the dirt in his garden area. Pulling weeds and tilling the ground gave him great pleasure. The smells of the fresh-turned dirt always made it feel more like spring. Ever since he could remember, they'd had a small garden on the land; after all, there was a little over twelve acres. Living by himself in the big house, he hadn't change the tradition. Sure, he'd cut back from planting too much. If there was extra, he always took it to his brother's or sister's place.

He had a few apple and pear trees that lined the small garden area. Looking around, he could see that they were starting to bloom. There were two rows of grapes that he always enjoyed. He'd even thought about adding another row or two to see if he could make his own wine. He'd gone online and found a great starter wine recipe that he really wanted to try his hand at.

He loved cooking, but he especially loved to pull his own fresh vegetables and fruit from his backyard and cook with them. Most people couldn't tell the difference, but with his heightened sense of smells and taste, he could easily pick out his own grown foods over store bought every time. He had a larger herb garden to the side. He loved to take fresh herbs into the restaurant to use when he cooked.

Todd often helped him with the garden. Iian thought it was because he liked to use the old tiller that he pulled behind Chester, Todd's huge black shire horse. His brother was weird when it came to pulling that big wooden thing behind the huge beast. Iian told him that he looked like a character off Little House on the Prairie. Todd told him that it was his way to get in touch with the past. Iian laughed at him and would sit back to watch the show. Iian preferred driving the John Deere they'd purchased the same year Todd had gotten the horse.

Now the barn sat empty since Todd had moved Chester to his newly renovated barn at his house. If the truth was known, Iian missed having the beast around. Maybe he'd get himself a horse, something he could ride through his fields on. Maybe even take down to the beach.

He wouldn't mind having a few horses. Maybe when he had kids he could teach them to ride.

He could just imagine his own kids; their blonde little heads, blue eyes, and a small dimple at the corner of their mouths when they smiled. Shaking his head, he realized the person he was thinking of as their mother. She was the only one he'd ever imagined having kids with.

He just needed to make sure to prove to her that his intentions were forever. He didn't want there to be any doubt in her mind that he wanted her to stay in Pride with him, in this house where she belonged.

She noticed a change in her mother since they had moved into the cabin. Her mother had changed, her mental state and even the way she dealt with small things had changed. It wasn't just the things she did in the middle of the night anymore. Once, Allison had been painting on the front porch and she'd been so engulfed with her work, she hadn't seen her mother walk by. An hour later, when she had gone inside, her mother was gone. She'd known true panic then.

The doctors had warned her about Alzheimer patients sometimes wondering off. Thoughts of terrible things ran through her head. First, she'd sprinted to the beach, in hopes that she had gone there. Then she'd thought about the woods. Had her mother walked there? Was she lost? Should she call someone? She rushed back to the cabin to double checked that she hadn't returned home, she picked up the phone and called Megan.

"Oh, your mother is here. I'm sorry, Allison, I should have called you when she arrived half an hour ago. I thought you knew." Megan sounded a little tense.

"Is everything alright?"

"Yes, yes, she's fine. She's rocking Sara out on the front porch. I'm truly sorry, Ally. I should have known to call you."

"Please don't worry. It's not your fault. She must have walked right by me. I don't know what I'm going to do. I guess I need to put a bell around her neck."

121

They both laughed.

The second time her mother wondered off had been just as stressful.

It was the fact that Allison hadn't gotten a full night's sleep since she'd brought her mother to the cabin that really concerned her. Was she destined to live this way forever? Being woken every night by her mother was extremely difficult and very stressful. She couldn't relax. When she showered, she was concerned her mother would wander off.

Even when she was at work, she was worried that her mother was causing problems. Megan had been overly gracious in having her mother stay with her during the days since they'd moved into the cabins. It was a relief knowing that her friend enjoyed spending time with her.

Megan kept assuring her that her mother was a great help with the guests and her children. She'd claimed that she hadn't had any little episodes while staying with them, but Ally wondered if she was just being kind to protect her.

But her final decision came on a stormy night less than two weeks after the fire.

They had been over at Todd and Megan's for dinner. Iian, Lacey, and Aaron had all been there as well. It had been such a lovely family dinner that when she and her mother had walked home, Allison's head had been comfortably numb.

After reaching their cabin, Allison decided to take a hot bath.

Ten minutes into her bath, she heard a crash. Pulling on her robe, she went to find her mother. Her mother stood in the living room looking around with huge eyes.

"Mom?" She approached her slowly. "Mom are you okay?"

Her mother spun around quickly and yelled, "Who are you? How did you get in here?"

Taking a step back, she held out her hands to her mother.

"Mom, it's me, Ally."

"Where are Dean and Steve? I don't remember how I got here? Where are my brothers? I want my brothers."

Dean and Steve were Allison's uncles. Dean had died in Vietnam before Allison had been born. Steve was retired and living in Florida with his wife of thirty years and their two children.

"Mom, it's okay. I'm here. It's me, Ally." She tried to step forward.

"Don't! I want to go home! I don't want to be here." Her mother took a step for the door.

What would she do if her mother took off? Run after her in the rain in her bathrobe? Trying to think ahead, she saw her sandals by the front door. If she had to, she could quickly put those on.

If her mother did take off, short of tackling her, she didn't know how she would convince her to come back to the house.

"Mom, we're in Megan's cabins. Remember the fire? We moved here a few weeks back. Remember you get to spend time with Matthew and Sara?" Allison reached into her mind to think of things her mother would enjoy hearing.

That stopped her backward shuffle towards the front door and she blinked a few times.

"The baby? Where did I put the baby?" Her mother looked around the room frantically.

"It's okay, the baby is with Megan. She's safe. Mom?"

"The baby is safe?"

"Mom?"

"Shh," her mother held her finger over her lips. "You'll wake the baby," she whispered in a stern voice.

She knew it was time to make finding a place for her mother her main focus, at least until she could figure out a more permanent living situation.

The next day, she'd driven into town and talked to Dr. Stevens about it. She'd even talked to several of the elders in town about the best place for her mother to be. Everyone pointed her to one place: the Hotel just outside of Edgeview. The Hotel was a retirement home and according to several people she'd talked to, it was the most qualified to help her mother out. They all claimed it was the cleanest, friendliest place.

Sitting outside the old building, she started second-guessing herself. There was a large sign that hung on the two-story brick building that said: *"The Hotel"* in large gold letters. Looking at the place it looked more like an old high school than a retirement home. The building was well maintained, the grounds were nicely groomed, and the place looked very friendly. The fact that there weren't old people sitting out front or even walking around out front, concerned her. Maybe it was nap time? Maybe everyone was inside playing bingo?

Taking a deep breath, she told herself it was just the

first place she was checking out. No decisions had to be made today.

When she entered the double doors, she noticed several things. First, there was an actual lobby desk, much like a hotel would have right up front. Second, a friendly, darker woman sat behind the counter, she wore a starched white shirt. Her smiled spread wide as Allison approached her. There was a beautiful display of flowers on a large table next to two bright red comfortable-looking couches. It looked like a lobby, sounded like a lobby, and even smelled like a lobby of a high rated hotel.

"You must be Allison Adams," the woman said, standing up and holding her hand out. Allison approached her and took the woman's hand in a friendly shake.

"Yes, I'm here to meet with Mrs. Sims."

"That's just fine. You have yourself a seat over there and I'll ring her right up. Do you want some coffee, soda, or water?"

"No, I'm fine, thank you," Allison said and took a seat on the couch facing a large stone fireplace. Less than two minutes later, a shorter woman in a dark suit walked into the room.

"Hello, I'm Stephanie Sims." After shaking Allison's hand, she said, "Would you like to take a tour?"

"Yes, please. I have some questions."

"Please, ask away."

Allison followed Mrs. Sims to an older elevator. The brass doors slid open quietly.

Once inside, Allison noted that the facade was completed with elevator music.

"Where is everyone?" Allison blurted out once the doors closed.

"Oh," Mrs. Sims laughed. "We don't have them locked up. Most everyone spends time upstairs or out back. The building used to be split into several other businesses. The second floor of the building is actually on the ground level out back. We have a wonderful garden and deck area that everyone enjoys. All the tenants live upstairs since it's cozier to be around other people. The downstairs is mainly for visitors and large group events such as Bingo, dances, and parties."

The doors slid open and they stepped out. There was a long hallway that opened up to a large room near the end. Allison noticed a nurses' station and saw two middle-aged women in cream-colored nurse outfits. They were busy behind the countertop, but both looked up and smiled as they walked by.

Then Allison followed Mrs. Sims down the hallway and turned to the left. The hallway opened up to a larger room with a wall of windows. The windows had a view of a beautiful, lush green garden which overlooked the old part of town and just beyond that was the most breathtaking view of the ocean. Older people of all different races and ages lounged about either inside the room or sat just outside under colorful umbrellas.

Two hours later, Allison walked back to her car with a smile on her face and a huge weight lifted from her heart.

Having the experience of sitting and talking to everyone who lived at the Hotel, helped ease her mind about her decision. Her time there made her appreciate her mother even more. Everyone was so happy and friendly.

The short drive to Megan's allowed her to sort through several things in her mind. Mrs. Sims wanted to meet with her mother tomorrow. They had a wonderful room available for her. The room was larger than the one she was now staying in, with a view that overlooked the back garden on top of it. The medical benefits of the staff and being close to the hospital couldn't be overlooked either. Having a staff that was there twenty-four-seven was invaluable.

When she drove up to the house and parked her car next to Megan's jeep, she stopped and watched her mother rocking Sara on the front porch swing.

Opening her door, she could hear her mother singing to the sleeping baby. She didn't want to disturb the wonderful sight, so she just leaned back on her car hood and closed her eyes. Remembering.

She must have been five or six and she'd had a bad day at school. One of the kids had told her that her drawing of a duck looked more like a big yellow doodie. This news had crushed Allison.

She'd run home after school and straight into her mother's waiting arms.

The song was more than a soothing song, it was a memory she wanted to hold onto for the rest of her life. One she'd hoped her children would enjoy. Knowing she'd taken a step today to help keep that dream alive, she stepped onto the front porch and sat next to her mother.

"She's so precious, so small. Much like you were at this age." Her mother continued to rock and hold the child.

Smiling over at her mom, she watched as Megan walked out the front door.

"Oh, Allison, I didn't hear you drive up. Here Teresa, let me take her from you."

"Oh, do you have to?"

Smiling, Megan walked over and took her sleeping child.

"I'll just go lay her down and be right back. Allison, do you want some tea?"

"No, I'm fine. Thank you for letting my mother stay here."

"No problem, she was an enormous help today."

When Megan disappeared through the door, she looked over to her mother.

"I just visited the most wonderful place. Mom, how would you like to stay at a fancy hotel in Edgeview?"

Lacey Stevens felt fat and miserable. How could women say they enjoyed being pregnant? Oh, it had its moments. Like when Jr., as she liked to call her unborn baby, would kick. The baby was also a great excuse for eating a second helping of dessert. Right now as she sat on her back porch watching her two dogs, Cleo and Bernard, run circles in the backyard, she just felt miserable. And she still had a month to go.

She remembered when Megan had been pregnant. She'd looked radiant. Of course, Megan was a lot taller than her own five-foot-four-inch frame. Megan had truly glowed, where Lacey felt like her pregnancy light had never come on. Sure, everyone told her that she glowed, but she just couldn't see it. Her husband had assured her that he found her very sexy still and he showed her every chance he could.

She was wearing one of her spring dresses, which in her mind reminded her of a fat woman's mu-mu. On her feet, she looked down and realized she couldn't see them, were a pair of Aaron's old flip-flops. His feet were almost ten sizes bigger than her petite six-and-a-half-sized feet. Now she knew, even if she couldn't see them, that her swollen feet rolled over the edges.

Taking a deep breath, she tried to relax. She didn't even budge when she heard the front door open and close.

"Lacey? It's Megan. Where are you?"

"Back here," she called out to her sister-in-law. Really, she thought of Megan more as a sister and even called her such most of the time.

"What are your plans for the day?" Megan came and sat beside her in the other lawn chair. She noticed how thin she was looking in her spring shorts and top and instantly felt jealous.

"Well, I was going to try to make it down to the restaurant to see if I could finish some paperwork that I know my brother has been avoiding." She tried to sit up a little bit but ended up relaxing back in the chair instead.

"I was wondering if you could watch the kids for me today. I have a few errands I needed to take care of for the B and B and didn't want to have to drag them along."

"Oh, I would love to," her prospects for the day just brightened. "Are they out in the car?"

"No, they're at home, Todd's still there. He's got a few meetings around eleven. Can you drive yourself over? Or do you need me to…" She broke off at Lacey's look. "Okay, okay. I get it. You can drive yourself," she smiled. "I won't be long." She stood and kissed her sister's cheek. "Thanks so much. See you around two."

When Lacey arrived at Megan and Todd's place, she

had changed into a pair of black leggings and a bright yellow top, which had cheered her up some.

Traversing the porch stairs took some doing, but she managed to climb them and was a little out of breath at the top. When was this kid going to come out?

Opening the door, which hadn't been locked in years, she almost peed her pants.

"Surprise!" everyone screamed. Megan, Allison, Todd, Iian, and over three dozen women of all ages jumped out at her in the hallway.

"What?" In all the years Lacey had been living in this town, this was the first time she'd been truly oblivious to something that was going on.

Megan walked up to her and hugged her. "Welcome to your baby shower. I'm just paying you back for my surprise shower. Did you think we'd forget you?"

"No...well, yes, well..." Lacey was speechless. "I hadn't even thought about it. I guess I've been so preoccupied with when this kid is going to come out, I totally forgot about having a shower."

Everyone laughed.

Allison really enjoyed her time at her friend's baby shower as she sat and talked to a few friends she hadn't seen in a while. It seemed it was a Jordan tradition to not know ahead of time the sex of the baby you were having. The baby gifts and decorations all varied in colors and she'd enjoyed buying a unisex outfit for the baby. She'd even purchased a large stuffed elephant to go along with it.

It felt good to sit in a crowded room full of people she

knew. After the initial surprise, Todd and Iian had quickly made excuses and left. She thought it was because they didn't want to be in a house with so many women.

The party wound down and after a few hours, the only remaining people were herself, Megan, and Lacey. Megan's kids had been moved upstairs for nap time. Lacey was sitting on the couch with her feet up on an ottoman, her gifts spread out around her. Allison thought she saw her friends head droop a few times, so she quietly went to help Megan clean up in the kitchen.

"I had a wonderful time today. I think we surprised her, don't you?" She asked while drying a large platter.

"Oh, I loved the look on her face. You know that's the first time I've seen her looked surprised." Megan chuckled.

Allison laughed, "I remember once when Abby and I had tried to scare her when she was babysitting. She'd just put us to bed and we'd hidden our Halloween masks under our blankets. So, when she came to check up on us, we jumped out from under the bed screaming." She chuckled with the memory.

"What did she do?"

"She calmly stated that if the two monsters didn't get back in bed, she wouldn't bring her Barbie house and car over the next time she babysat. She hadn't even blinked. It's funny how she and Iian have that extra sense to know what's going on." Letting out a sigh at the thought of Iian, she tried to cover the heat that seeped into her face.

"Girl," Megan said, smiling, "you don't have to hide it from me. I may not have the extra senses that Lacey and Iian have, but I can tell there's something between you two."

She smiled over at her friend. "I think the whole town knows it. I just wish I'd get a better feeling of what he thought of me. I just have to decide what I think of him. I mean, I've had this thing for him for as long as I can remember."

Turning around, Allison leaned against the countertop. "You know life is short. If there is anything to learn about by what my mother is going through, it's that I need to enjoy what I have, when I have it. I can't deny that I'd love to have a relationship with him. I just want to make sure it's right for us."

"It'll come. The answers *will* come. If it takes a little time, just sit back and enjoy what happens, when it does." She turned to her friend. "I'm glad you helped me with this party. You really do have a great eye for decorating. Come on, let's go sit outside and enjoy the peace and quiet. At least until either the kids wake up or Lacey does." They both laughed.

CHAPTER 11

*L*ess than a week later, Allison sat with her mother on her newly purchased daybed in her new room at the Hotel. Megan had gone with them to purchase the bed, an oak nightstand, and a dresser. Later, she and her mother had gone to Walmart in Edgeview and purchased a large flat-screen television for her new room. Her mother had picked out the new linens and towels, all the time explaining how excited she was that Allison was finally moving out. Not once did her mother comprehend what was going on. She'd explained it several times and each time she had to start from the beginning.

Now they sat in the freshly decorated room.

Her mother looked at her and said, "It's so wonderful here. I can't believe you got me such a wonderful room. How long did you say I would be staying?"

"Mom, this is your new room. You're going to be living here now. Remember?"

"Well, I think it's just wonderful. Everyone is so friendly. It's such a nice place. I never want to leave."

~

Iian was outside his house, working in his garden area off the back patio when he noticed a shadow over him. It caught him off guard, and he hated being caught off guard. The man stood in a dark brown outfit and held out a clipboard. Iian read his lips.

"So, if you'd just sign here we can get started."

"I'm sorry," Iian stood, dusting off his hands. "I'm deaf, could you please repeat what you said?" He hated the look that others, who didn't know him, always gave. First, it was always shocking and then they would get embarrassed like they'd done something wrong. They always ended up with a pitying look.

"I'm sorry. I'm from Brandon's Furniture. We're delivering your new furniture. If you'd just sign here, we can start unloading the truck."

Iian had ordered the furniture for the bedrooms upstairs. A lot of what had been up there was outdated and in need of replacing. So, he'd gotten on his laptop and in the process had found out that he loved ordering online. He had enjoyed taking his time picking out what would go in each room. He'd even ordered himself a few items for his kitchen.

He was spending quite a lot of his inheritance on fixing up the place. After all, he hadn't touched any of the money since he'd turned twenty and had been given full rein to do so. He figured his father would've approved of all the improvements he'd been making. Iian made enough at the restaurant to live comfortably and didn't usually bother with the extra money that sat in his accounts. He also hadn't touched his income from the other family business, Jordan Shipping, which Todd ran full time.

Two hours later, he had sweat rolling down his back between his shoulders. He'd moved everything around until he was completely satisfied with the outcome. Gone were the little kids' rooms, and in their place were two guest bedrooms and the most professional art studio he'd ever seen. He stood back and smiled at the outcome.

The light-colored walls were still bare, but he could just imagine hanging some art in different places. The furniture was light oak and had simple lines, which kept with the flow of some of the older pieces he had. He'd kept the large bay windows uncovered. He liked the light that came in through them. The view in this room was the best in the house. His bluff stood a few yards out and he noticed that today the ocean was a peaceful blue with a matching sky.

The other rooms, his and Todd's old bedrooms, were outfitted with their own unique furniture.

Smiling to himself, he thought that the only thing missing was someone to help fill the emptiness. Grabbing up his coat, he decided an evening walk would help him think of how he'd get Allison where he wanted her.

Driving home felt lonely. Her mother had looked like she was enjoying herself playing Bingo, but still, the worry played in the back of her mind. Had she done the right thing? She felt like a mother leaving her child at school for the first time. Was her mother going to play nice with the other people? Would she have a freak-out moment? She knew the staff was well equipped to handle her mother's condition, but still, she couldn't help worrying.

When she parked in her spot, she could see the bright lights coming from the main house and knew it was dinner time. Most of the guests at the bed and breakfast were enjoying their dinner there. Not wanting to be around the crowd, she started walking towards her cabin on the dimly-lit pathway.

It had been a cool cloudy day and the sun never really had made an appearance. Here in the trees, it was even darker and gloomier looking. She'd made it almost halfway to her cabin when she heard a sound behind her. Turning around, she thought she would see another guest walking the path. But there wasn't anyone there and the sound had stopped. She turned and proceeded down the pathway until she heard it again.

This time it was faster and louder. Spinning around she braced herself, but again, no one was there. Looking around slowly, she could only see darkness in the trees. Her breathing was starting to come faster, and she could hear no normal sounds coming from the trees, no birds, no crickets, no frogs, nothing. Just an eerie silence. Cautiously, she turned and picked up her pace, glancing over her shoulder occasionally. When her cabin came into sight, she rushed to the front porch and hastily opened the door with her key. Slamming the door shut, she made sure to flip the lock quickly. Leaning back against it, she realized she was out of breath and her heart was racing. Had it been an animal? Was someone following her?

Just then her phone rang causing her to jump almost a foot off the ground and let out a small squeal. With her hand over her heart, she went to answer it.

Fifteen minutes later, she was shaking and out of breath for different reasons. Long gone was the feeling that someone had followed her. Instead, it was replaced by the worry and questions she had about her future.

She had some thinking to do. Looking out the large front windows of the cabin, she decided a long walk on the beach might help clear her mind. Even though it was still gloomy, she thought the cool air would help clear her mind.

Grabbing up her jacket, she headed out the door to take the pebble path through the tall grass which opened up to the sandy Oregon shore. Large chunks of driftwood lay scattered across the empty beach.

The summer weather had finally settled in leaving most days warmer, but the breeze off the water was still cool enough. Looking off to the horizon, she could see large dark clouds. It appeared there would be a storm later that night. Keeping her head down, she walked along the shore and did her thinking.

Iian stood on his cliff; he watched the rain forming far off in the horizon and knew a storm was coming. Usually, the weather could take a few hours to reach land or just a few minutes. Living on the coast his whole life, he learned he could usually gauge it pretty well. This one, he thought, might hit the shore before he could make it back to the safety of his house. So, he'd get wet. Living in Oregon, you learned to either love it or hate it. He loved it.

Then he saw her. At first glance, she appeared to be just a dot on the horizon, but he could tell it was her. He would always be able to tell it was her from afar. Her head was down, the hood of her bright red windbreaker covered her hair and face. It was the way she walked that set her apart from anyone else. She carried herself like a dancer most of the time, but when she was deep in thought, she tended to march as she was doing now.

He took a path that would take him to the beach before she passed the cliffs he frequented. He knew she hadn't seen or heard him, even though he had dislodged a truckload of pebbles and dirt getting down the hill.

Coming up behind her, he easily matched his pace with her brisk one.

"Heading somewhere?" He asked.

She jumped and then whirled around putting her hand up to her heart. Her face was flushed from the brisk walk and the tip of her nose was a bright pink. No doubt from the cool wind.

"Oh," she said. He watched her lovely mouth make the all-too-familiar word.

It took Allison several seconds to realize where she was. She hadn't intended on going this far up the beach. Looking around, she realized she was past the bluff. How could she have gone this far and not known it?

Blinking, she looked at Iian and said, "Wow, I guess I walked farther than I intended." She tried for casual.

He signed as he spoke, mostly out of habit. "Doing some deep thinking?" He took her hand in his and started pulling them up the path to his house.

His hand was warm, and she could feel his heartbeat in

her palm. Turning her head so he could read her lips, she said, "Yes, well…"

"Hang on," he interrupted, "let's get out of the rain." He saw her surprise when the heavens chose that moment to open up and drench both of them. Smiling, he continued to pull her up the hill.

Quickly walking beside, him, she kept her hand in his as he guided them through the rocky path lined with tall grass. The rain was cold, and she realized the breeze was blowing the wind right through her light windbreaker.

All of a sudden, she was very glad he'd come along when he did. She hadn't been focused on the weather and the thought of being stuck on the beach in a storm gave her the chills. She'd grown up here and knew better than to go marching down the beach and not pay attention to the skies.

When they reached the back door of his house, he pulled her into the kitchen and reluctantly let go of her hand to help pull off her wet jacket. Then he pulled his own coat off and hung them on the hook on the laundry room wall.

She was rubbing her hands up and down her arms, trying to get warm when he turned back around.

"Come on, let's go into the living room. I'll get a fire going." Walking into the next room he looked back as she followed him slowly.

She watched him walking into the next room. This was the first time she'd been in the large brick house. She'd seen it from the beach ever since she could remember. It always looked like a large castle shining on the hills above the beach. From her old bedroom window, she could just make out the brown roof poking up through the trees.

Following him out of the large kitchen, she watched his back and enjoyed the view. He had always been very tall, but it wasn't until high school that his shoulders had become so broad. He had played basketball all throughout junior high and high school, and she'd played on the girl's team herself. Admitting it only once to her sister, the only reason she had tried out for the team was that she knew Iian had already made the boys team.

When she walked into the large living room, she noticed that he hadn't bothered to turn on the lights. She saw him bent over the fireplace, his shirt and jeans were wet from the rain. Looking down at herself, she realized she too was drenched. Her white shirt clung to her skin. Quickly, while his back was turned, she tried to pull it loose and crossed her arms over her front.

Walking further into the dim room, she looked around. Even shadowed in darkness, she could tell it was decorated in warm colors and felt very comfortable. Iian finished lighting the fire and turned back to her.

"Come over here, you must be cold." He still signed along as he spoke. She found it interesting to watch his hands. Could she really be turned on by just watching his hands?

Signing back, she said, "Thank you, I didn't realize the storm was coming that fast. I don't know what I would have done if you hadn't come along." She stayed where she was, not wanting to get any closer to him. "I guess I would have gotten even wetter."

"How's your mom?" He walked towards her. No, more like stalked towards her.

When he reached her, he grabbed her hand and pulled

her lightly towards the fire. He had a funny look on his face and she noticed that his fingers were warm in hers.

"She's, she's fine. I think she really enjoys the staff and the people at the home. I'm just nervous since it's her first night there." He had pulled her down to the couch and sat close to her. It was so very hard to focus on anything when he was looking at her like that.

"What caused you to be out on the beach so late tonight?"

She took a large breath and released it. "I've been offered a position at a top art institute."

"Wow, congratulations." He could tell by the look on her face that there was something more. "And?"

"It's in Paris."

The room was silent.

"I don't know if I want to pick up and move. I know everything I had was lost in the fire. To be honest, I was very glad I'd come home when I did. It wasn't just for a visit you know. I'd come home to stay." She leaned further back in the warmth of the couch. "It's not that I didn't enjoy California, it's just that I was done with that life-style. I thought I would eventually get used to living in a large city. But Paris?"

She'd leaned so far back that the firelight no longer lit up her face. He took her hand and pulled her towards him and the light, so he could see her face more clearly.

Realizing it had been too dark away from the fire and he couldn't read her lips, she blushed. He just smiled back at her.

"What do you want to do?" He asked.

"I'm not too sure of that myself. I know I couldn't be

happy half-way around the world when my mother is… is…" she shrugged her shoulders.

"I've always thought you would look like this in the firelight," he said softly.

She just looked at him confused.

"Beautiful." He reached out and toyed with the ends of her hair. "I've been wanting to see if it was as soft as I imagined."

"Iian," it came out as a whisper and she realized nothing else really mattered.

"Allison, there's something I've been holding back for years. I don't know how much longer I can hold it at bay."

"Iian, I think," she moistened her lips and heard him groan. Looking at him, she realized his eyes were fixed on her lips. Which naturally caused her to look at his. They looked very inviting. She loved looking at the small cleft in his chin and imagined playing her tongue over the sweet dip.

"I think," she said again and then thought, screw it! You only live once. Right? Taking a deep breath, she leaned forward and rubbed her lips gently over his.

CHAPTER 12

*H*e was transfixed by her mouth. He could feel himself shaking with want. His palms started to sweat and there was a slight dimness in his vision. Allison was the only light he could see. Her hair was wet as he rubbed it carefully between his fingers. Her face was still flushed from the cold weather and the brisk walk, which caused her blue eyes to stand out more. When her tongue dipped outside to moisten her bottom lip, he tried to hold back a groan. Then she was kissing him and the softness of her overwhelmed him.

He should have known he was on dangerous ground when he'd seen her walking on the beach. He should have hustled her back home instead of bringing her into a fire-lit room and sitting in the dark with her. He sunk his fingers into her soft hair and explored her warm mouth, realizing he could happily die a content man in her arms.

Reaching up, he explored her cool skin under her wet shirt. Pulling it aside, he marveled at the little bumps that rose when he placed his mouth where his hands had just been. He loved the taste of her.

He had experience with women before and after his accident, but nothing had prepared him for this, for her. He pulled the wet garment higher, exposing white cotton that was not only practical but very feminine. He could feel her tense and looked up into her eyes.

"Say that you'll stay here, in my house, in my bed." When she nodded her head yes, he picked her up with a laugh. She held onto his shoulders and ran soft, timid kisses up his neck as he carried her up the stairs quickly. He made it to the end of the hallway in record time. She was light and felt just right in his arms.

Kicking the door closed with his foot, he walked across the room as he started kissing that sweet mouth of hers again. Stopping a foot from the bed, he knew he wanted to savor every moment, but she was heating him up so fast. He thought he couldn't wait, didn't want to wait. Pulling back, he looked at her.

"Open your eyes Ally, I want to see you," he said. She tilted her head and slowly opened her lids. Her blue eyes, which were normally focused on anything and everything, had gone cloudy. Her cheeks were pink, her lips tilted up slightly, exposing the little dimple at the corner of her mouth. When her tongue came out to wet her lips again, he watched the movement with wonder.

She ran her hands up his wet t-shirt, pulling it up and off, exposing his chest to her view.

Her eyes ran up and down his powerful chest and arms. He too had little bumps rising all over his chilled skin. Bending her head, she ran her tongue over his damp skin and tasted him. Then she ran her tongue over his taught nipple and nibbled ever so lightly as he moaned.

He watched every move she made, and when she looked up at him, he smiled. He was trying to calm the massive desire he had for her, at least slow it down to a reasonable pace. Smiling, she started to move across his chest to do the same to his other nipple, but he reached down and removed her wet t-shirt with quick movements.

Then when she was exposed, he placed his hands under her arms again, this time lifting her and tossing her on the large bed. She hit the soft mattress with a slight bounce and laughed.

Then he was next to her, taking his turn licking his way across her skin. He ran his mouth down over her soft stomach. His tongue ran a trail just above her plain, white bra.

Running her fingers through his wet curly hair was another pleasure she marveled in. Holding his head to her as he feasted and pulled the light material aside, she too let out a moan, one he felt with his large hand that was spread out over her tight stomach. He was running his mouth over her, gently playing with each of her ribs. Then when he started to go lower, he hit her tickle spot and she jolted upright, grabbing for him.

Looking up quickly, he saw the smile and concern on her face. It took him less than a second to realize what a piece of gold he'd unearthed.

"Tickle spot, eh?" he said, trying to pull his hand free.

"Oh, no you don't, Iian..." She tried to push his hand away. With his hands clamped in hers, he ducked his head and licked the spot slowly. She released his hands and grabbed his head, trying to dislodge him from the spot. He kept running his tongue slowly over and over her, until she was holding his head down, instead of trying to pull him away. The laugh and smile on her face slowly faded into something stronger-want.

With his hands released, he continued running them over her, learning her much like a blind man would read braille. Then when his hands dipped and unbuckled her jeans, she helped him slide the wet denim down her chilled legs. She reached for his pants, but he slid away, holding himself above her. His eyes ran up her. She'd never been embarrassed by her body, she knew how she looked. When he smiled at her and mouthed "Beautiful," she smiled at him.

"Iian, please," she said as he watched her lips move. When she reached for him, he pulled her hands into one of his and held them next to her head.

"Let me, Ally, I want to savor you." He dipped his head again, returning on his previous journey down her body. This time, when he reached her tickle spot, she tightened just a little, but then relaxed as he skipped over the spot to continue his downward journey.

With her hands released, she played her fingers over his taut muscles in his shoulders.

Finally, he reached the white lace that covered her. Gently, ever so gently, he pulled it aside to expose her to his view.

Never had she felt so much anticipation as she did while he looked at her. She could see the need and desire plainly in his eyes. Then when she thought she couldn't stand it any longer, he dipped his head and tasted just there. Her body heated, and she felt a shiver run down to her toes.

This time, her shoulders came off the mattress on their own accord. Her hands fell to the comforter and fisted there as he feasted on her. Never had she felt anything quite like the excitement of Iian's mouth on her. He'd obviously taken great care to know what women truly wanted. Using his fingers and mouth, he tortured her further. She twisted her fingers in the comforter and felt herself building to release.

Just when she thought she couldn't wait any longer, he stood, and in one quick motion, removed his own boots and jeans. Basking in the lines and firmness of him, she watched him reach over, pulling something out of the nightstand. The light was dim enough, but she could just make out the flash of foil as he placed a condom wrapper on the bed.

Then he was beside her and kissing her until her head was spinning again. She thought it would be speed from here. After all, she'd seen his erection and knew his balls were so tight that it was probably painful. He continued to kiss her and run his hands up and down her naked body slowly.

She too was running her hands over him. Taking a chance, she reached down and lightly placed her fingers around him, gently running up and down until he pulled her hand up and away. Cuffing them in his own above her head again. He looked down at her and just shook his head as he smiled. Then he licked her lips and nibbled on her bottom lip until she was squirming.

Trying a different tactic, she pushed her hips upwards and started grinding them against his hard, naked thigh.

This only heightened her own excitement and almost caused her to come against him.

"Please Iian," she moaned, but his head was busy back at her breast. How could he have so much self-control? Didn't he know she was ready to burst?

Finally, she saw an opening. He'd released her hands and was halfway on his side, slowly edging his way back down her body. She noticed that he was off center and doing her best wrestling move, flipped him over and had him on his back in two seconds flat. He smiled up at her as if he'd planned the whole thing. She sat straddling him smiling back down at him.

"You think this is funny?" she signed to him. "You want to torture me? I'll show you how to torture someone."

She held his arms down and mouthed, "Don't move!" She had just enough emotion behind her that he nodded his head in agreement.

Running her hands down from his wrists, she explored his forearms, his upper arms and enjoyed the veins that bulged in his triceps. Then dipping her head, she ran her tongue down the same path.

She'd always admired his body, but had never truly seen it up close, this naked, or tasted it like she was doing now. He had his own unique taste and she marveled in the sweetness of him. How could a man taste so good?

Looking at her hands, she realized just how wide his chest was. The muscles that tensed as she explored him made her smile. Running her fingers, ever so lightly down his stomach, she followed the light cover of hair that trailed downwards to his erection. Using her fingers, she cuffed him and ran her tongue over the head and explored the length and girth of him. She always found it such a wonder at how a man could be strong and yet so soft feeling at the same time. Like rose petals over steel.

She could honestly say that Iian was larger than anyone else she'd experienced. She thought it better to keep that little secret to herself. Smiling as she heard him groan again, she figured she would just have her revenge on him, but after a moment, she lost herself in the pleasure of pleasing him.

Then she was being tossed back on her back and he was hovering above her. This time, his eyes were dark, and his face was set in concentration.

She'd never seen him look so... so. She got no further in her thoughts because in one quick move, he was inside her and she arched off the bed and gasped his name. Then it was all speed and power.

Never before had he shown such restraint. He'd wanted to explore and remember every part of her. He didn't know that by doing so, he'd torture himself to the point of pain. Then she'd flipped him over and tried to do the same. How could she know that he'd been on the verge of coming before she ran her hands over him, her tongue over him? Then her mouth had been on him and he'd had to recite all the spices he could think of until finally, he'd been so caught up in her, he had to have her.

When he'd driven into her heat, he was sure he wouldn't last long, but the more he had her, the more he wanted to hold himself at bay. She was so wet, hot, and tight he enjoyed every second. He could just lose himself.

He loved the way she moved with him. The way she smelled. Everything about her was perfection.

When her hands had reached around him and held tight to his hips, he felt her nails skim his skin and smiled. He looked down at her face. Her eyes were closed, and her mouth was slightly opened. He could see the moment she exploded around him.

Knowing he could build her up again, he pulled one of her legs tight against him and watched her begin to rise. Just when he saw her about to go over the edge a second time, he joined her.

He lay there feeling her chest rise and fall against his own. Her soft skin felt like heaven next to his. She fit perfectly in his arms. She *felt* perfect in his arms. Why had he waited so long to finally get her here? How was he going to make sure she stayed here?

The rain was still coming down hard when she surfaced. She was being pressed deep into the soft mattress. Iian's weight was pinning her and keeping her warm at the same time.

The room, which had been overly hot when they'd been enjoying each other, had quickly cooled her already damp skin. Reaching around, she tried to pull the comforter over them both. He shifted and rolled them both until she thought they'd hit the floor. Then he shifted, and the comforter was over them as he rolled them back to the middle of the large bed.

"Tell me you're not moving to Paris. Tell me you're going to stay right here," he mumbled against her hair.

Nodding her head in agreement, she smiled and snuggled into his warm chest to settle in for the night as he played his hand lightly over her hair.

When he could tell she was asleep, he closed his eyes and, smelling her wonderful scent, drifted off.

CHAPTER 13

*G*eorge *Jordan stood on the deck of his sailboat
and noticed it was taking on water fast. His feet
were spread wide, the stance of a man who'd
been born a sailor. The heavy waves crashed into the
boat's small hull. It wasn't the rain or the water leaking
into the boat that concerned him, it was the lightning that
kept getting closer and closer, along with the large wall of
dark clouds he knew would hit them soon.*

Looking over at his son, he watched as he helped hoist
the sails, expertly. He saw the fear in his eyes. He remembered seeing that face for the first time, eighteen years ago.
At birth, his youngest son had reminded him of a fish out
of the water. He'd gasped for breath and then cried out
with a strong voice, his big blue eyes looked around the
room, searching for a means to his first meal, not knowing
his mother had given her life for his.

Taking hold of the ropes, he swung the mast around
and headed in the direction he knew would be land.
Although it was in the middle of the day, the dark sky

didn't show any signs of light. He'd been born on the water, made a living off it, and even raised his three kids to respect and love it. Now it appeared, it was going to be the death of him. Well, at least he'd do everything in his power to make sure it didn't take his son along.

The Dawn-treader was his favorite sailboat. Looking up at the mast, he laughed as the sail caught a large gust of wind and started to pull the vessel towards life. Knowing it wouldn't be enough – it couldn't be enough – he smiled at his son, who was holding onto the side of the boat tightly.

"We're moving, you just hold tight. I promised your mom on the day you were born I'd take care of you, and I'll be damned if I let a little storm come between me and my promise."

A few minutes later, the strong winds had started to crack the mast in half. He could hear the wood creaking under the weight of the wind. A few more minutes and the tiny vessel shook hard, almost throwing them both overboard. Then it started to tip to the side and take its last dip towards a dark, watery grave.

"Come on my boy, it's time to go," he shouted over the wind.

Lightning cracked, causing his son's face to be illuminated. He could see the fear mirrored in his silvery eyes. Looking overboard towards the small dinghy that was tied to the back, he yelled over the wind, "Grab hold and don't let go when you land. Just you remember that, don't let go! I love you son."

He pushed his son with all his might and watched as he jumped across the empty space between the two boats. His son landed in the dinghy with a thud. When his son shook his head and look back to him, he was just about to jump into the icy water and make a swim for it, when everything went dark.

Iian watched from the small dinghy as his father and the boat exploded with light. The last thing he'd ever hear in his life was "I love you, son."

~

She'd been trying to wake him for a few minutes. He'd woken her up with his moaning. Her legs had been wrapped around his and he'd kicked and thrashed about until she'd woken confused. Then she'd remembered where she was.

Trying to wake him up was hard. She'd called his name at first, then almost smacked herself in the forehead for her stupidity. Grabbing his shoulders, she began shaking him until his eyes flew open. He blinked a few times, then reached over and turned on a light on the nightstand.

"Are you okay?" she signed.

He just nodded his head and ran his hands over his face. When he looked back at her, she asked, "Was it about your father?"

He shook his head in agreement.

"Do you want to talk about it?"

His head was pounding like crazy and his vision was a little gray on the edges. A true sign that a migraine was quickly on its way.

"It comes in bursts. Sometimes all I need to do is have a certain smell or taste and there it is. The image of my father standing at the helm. Seeing him smiling down at me with the sky to his back." He shook his head. "When I have the dreams, they're almost always followed by migraines." He rubbed his temples. "I don't remember much, just leaving the dock the day before. Then at least in my dreams, there was a storm. I think it was the lightning that killed him. He'd pushed me onto the dinghy. The old man had always been strong. But he just picked me up and tossed me, not thinking of himself. When I hit, my head smacked the deck hard and everything went silent. I looked back over to him just as he exploded in light."

She ran her hands over his face and wiped away his tears.

"He threw me into the dinghy to save me and I laid there and watched him die. The last thing I heard was him telling me he loved me."

"Iian," she whispered and had a tear of her own falling down her cheek.

He signed back. "I'm sorry I woke you." He wiped the tear from her cheek. He looked over at the clock, which said it was still early enough that he thought about snuggling back down with her. Then he got a better look at her. She held the sheet close to her chest and he realized what she had on underneath, or the lack of what was underneath.

"Come here." He pulled her close. She looked wonderful and smelled even better. He ran his fingers over the sheet she held close to her chest. He saw her shiver, saw her skin start to glow with excitement. He watched her eyes fog over, she leaned her head back and he watched the light play across her face. He let his fingers linger before dipping them lower and gently pulled the sheet away, exposing more of her soft skin to his view. Her hand fell away and rested next to her on the bed. He could see her chest rise and fall with each breath.

Shifting his weight, he leaned down to kiss her, running his mouth along her slender neck. Playing his tongue across her shoulders, he went lower to enjoy the softness of her.

He removed the sheet completely so that she was fully exposed for his view. The low light played over her as he ran his fingers over her. She laid back and held very still as he took his time learning every curve, every soft spot.

His fingers slowly played over every inch of her. She moaned every time he would get closer and closer to her center. She felt herself vibrate with want. Grabbing the sheet beneath her, she closed her eyes as his mouth finally found the spot where she ached. He played a finger just over her tender nub, and she couldn't help but moan. He had a way with his mouth. Something was building deep inside her and she couldn't help but try to pull him closer. She wanted him deep inside her.

She twisted and tried to pull him up to her. Then he was there. His silver-blue eyes focused on her face, searching her own eyes. She smiled up at him and pulled him down for a kiss just as he entered her slowly.

"Please Iian," she pulled his face to hers, so he could read her plea. "I can't stand it, I need you."

Smiling down at her, "What? What do you want, Ally? Tell me."

"I want it fast." She closed her eyes again and pumped her hips trying to get him to move faster.

"Like this?" He pulled back until he hovered just outside her sleek entrance. He saw her physically moan and she tried to pull his hips back down to her. He chuckled when her nails dug into his hips.

Trying a different tactic, she ran her tongue slowly over her bottom lip. Two could play at this game, she thought. Running her fingers through his hair, she traced down his neck and smiled as he watched her mouth hungrily. Then she moved down his shoulders, down his chest, over his tight stomach. His muscles bunched as she glided over each one. She watched as his eyes closed and held himself very still above her. Then she went lower, circling him as he hovered at her entrance.

She played her finger over him and enjoyed the moist drop that appeared on the end. Then she tightened her grip around his girth and watched his eyes snap open. Finally, he plunged into her heat again and it was all speed. Each thrust took them deeper in pleasure. His hips pumped faster. All she could do was hold onto him and enjoy the speed she'd so much wanted.

Closing her eyes, she threw back her head as the feelings started to build deep inside her. Just before her release, she felt him waver. He drove deeper and harder and she could tell they would reach the end together.

She felt so good, he tried to hold still. Holding himself above her as he enjoyed watching her eyes fog. Never had he experienced the thrill of seeing pure pleasure cross her face. He held himself still until he felt her hips starting to pump against him. Then he began to move slowly. Her hands came up and grabbed at him, trying to get him to move faster. Her body came off the mattress, her hips moving in a rhythm on their own. He lost his control when she had shifted her hips, his mind had just shut off and all he could think about was pleasing her with speed.

Iian woke pinned down. At first, it took him a few seconds to realize Allison was lying across him, her hair spread out across his chest and face. If he opened his mouth, he would breathe it in and most likely choke. Reaching up, he brushed it off and enjoyed the softness. He could feel her steady breathing and rubbed his hand down her back and knew the moment she started to awake.

He woke hard, but when she started to stretch, he grew even more so. Looking over at the clock, he decided they had just enough time to shower.

Before she got the chance to fully wake up, he sat and pulled her with him. He carried her into the bathroom in his arms. Since they were both naked already, he just walked into the large glass enclosure and, still holding her, turned on the spray full blast. All twenty-odd shower heads sprayed cold water at them from every direction. No part of them went unnoticed by its spray, which was quickly warming up.

He was sure she was cussing at him. He could feel her body vibrating with anger and she was squirming in his hold. Her arms and legs kicked out to hit any part of him. He had to hold on extra tight to her since their bodies were slick with water.

When he finally allowed himself to look down at her and read her lips, most of her temper had run its course.

"And you kiss me with that mouth!" He chuckled as she punched his shoulder, which only bounced off his slick skin.

Setting her down on her feet, he reached for the

shampoo and dumped a hand full on top of her head. By now the water was warm enough that he knew she couldn't complain about the temperature anymore.

He started scrubbing her hair lightly, and when she reached up to take over, he swiped at her hand.

"I'm doing this, you just stand still and let me take care of you." He continued to rub her hair.

He watched her lower lip pout out and smiled as she continued to glare at him. He liked the length of her hair, the soft texture, the feel of it in his hands. He ran his fingers over her scalp and watched her eyes close as she started to relax.

Once he was done with her hair, he continued on a downward path. Using his soapy hands to rub her full breasts, he took great care to give each his full attention. Her head rolled back, and he watched her starting to sway. Pulling her over to the built-in tile seat, he motioned for her to sit. She blinked a few times, but then sat and watched as he hit a small button, which started a new set of heads spraying water on her back and legs. It was like a big Jacuzzi but in a shower.

He got another hand full of shampoo and continued his path of cleaning. Taking great care to wash each foot. He noticed when he hit another tickle spot just inside each of her insteps. Her legs were long and slim, and he enjoyed running his hands up each one, making sure to give them his full attention. Then he slid her bottom away from the back wall, so she sat on the edge of the seat. He gently spread her legs and with another handful of soap set to his task of cleaning and pleasing her.

~

She sat back and watched Iian work on cleaning her feet, his dark wet head bent over, focused on his task. She watched as he took great care with each toe. Only once did he hit a tickle spot and she tensed momentarily. He ran his soapy hands over her legs, and she moaned with pleasure as the tension was massaged from each muscle.

Then he pulled her bottom forward and he ran his fingers over her and she lost the ability to think. He took his time massaging her, slowly entering her with one finger then another, exploring her and massaging her inner muscles. She reached for his head as he lowered it and set his mouth to her softness. Her legs wrapped around his shoulders and she held on until she exploded with a shout of his name.

When she was totally relaxed on the seat, he looked up and kissed her deeply, then said against her lips, "Good morning."

She laughed and smiled at him. Standing up next to him, her hand traveled down his tight stomach muscles. She wrapped her fingers around his erection, squeezing ever so gently. With a wicked smile, she lowered herself and returned the morning favor.

A while longer, they stood under the spray together, cleaned and pleased.

"Next time you pull me from the bed and dump me in a shower, make sure it's warm first."

CHAPTER 14

*J*ian walked into work smiling. So, he was half an hour late. What good was it to own your own restaurant, if you couldn't show up late after having hot shower sex?

It wasn't until halfway through the day that he heard about Allison's problems with Kevin Williams. The whole town was quick to receive any gossip and he was always the last one to find out. He knew it was because everyone talked about everything. Most days, he tuned out reading lips if he knew it was gossip. When Lacey came in during lunch to pick up Aaron's order, she'd mention something about Kevin and he'd paid attention. He'd learned all about the scene outside the school.

Why hadn't she told him? It had been weeks since the scene. Everyone in town knew! Everyone but him. He started off upset, then he graduated to anger, and then settled on hurt. He knew that spending one night with her didn't entitle him to everything, but damn it, they were friends first. Why hadn't she told him about the problems she was having?

~

Allison had the day off, so she headed into Edgeview to get a few things and to visit her mother.

Her mother had been enjoying herself so much, her visit had seemed more like she was in the way. So she headed to Walmart and the small mall there to pick up some needed items.

She'd received her new driver's license in the mail several weeks back, along with all of her replacement credit cards. So of course, she had to buy a new purse. She'd gone to the art store as well since she had to replace most of her art supplies.

She was thankful that some of her more expensive art supplies had been left in the trunk of her car the day of the fire.

Lastly, she stopped by the small boutique that had lots of wonderful undergarments. Knowing all she had was the simple cotton bra and underwear she'd been given after the fire, she decided to take her time, picking out several nighties she thought Iian would enjoy. She'd also picked up a dozen or so new sexier underwear and bra sets.

Her hands were weighted down when she went back out to her car. It wasn't until she was a few feet away that she noticed the flat tire.

Now thinking about digging into her truck to get her spare out, she noticed the front tire was flat as well. Had she hit something on her way here? Her mind raced through her drive. Then she walked around the other side of her car and noticed those tires were flat as well. Setting down the bags, she walked over and bent down next to one. That's when she noticed the huge gash that ran the entire side of the tire. Going to each tire, she realized someone had done this on purpose.

Two hours and several hundred dollars later, she walked into her cabin. Gone was the joy of her shopping day. Instead, she was left with a bitter taste and an uneasy feeling. The tire place had called the Edgeview Police. They claimed it was standard when tires were slashed. She'd spent the entire time in the tire store on the phone with her insurance agent. After being assured that a check would be in the mail, she felt a small sense of relief. But still, she wondered, who would have done this? Did Edgeview have gangs that liked to go around slashing peoples tires? The local police assured her they didn't. Her mind quickly raced to thoughts of Kevin.

She'd just sat down after unloading her purchases when there was a knock on her door.

Seeing Iian on the other side of the front window lifted her spirits.

"Hello, come on in." She waved him into the room.

When he was inside, she suddenly realized how small the place was. He filled the room as he walked over and sat on the small couch.

"How was your day?" he asked. She hadn't changed anything in the place since moving in. Most of the items she'd received after the fire still sat in their boxes or were put away in the cupboards.

She sat next to him and proceeded to tell him about her car problems.

"Do you think it had anything to do with your problems with Kevin Williams?" he asked, she could see the tension in his face.

"My problems with Kevin Williams? What problems with Kevin Williams?"

"Why didn't you tell me you had a run in with him in the school parking lot? I had to hear it from my sister that he threatened you." He stood and started to pace the floor, which was actually quite funny to watch. Since he would take three steps, turn, and pace the other way. He did this a few times before she had to stop him by standing in front of him.

"How am I supposed to talk to you if you're pacing back and forth?" He stopped and looked at her. "I didn't tell you about my 'run-in' with Kevin Williams because I didn't give it a second thought. He'd just lost his wife and kids and he was drunk. There was nothing more to tell. I'm sure he's gotten over it and has enough to deal with his family problems."

She placed her hand on his shoulders. "Why are you so upset that I didn't tell you?" she asked.

He looked into her eyes. He wanted to gather her in his arms, but he wanted the whole story first. He saw the worry in her face and didn't like that she'd run into problems in Edgeview.

"Why didn't you call me when you found your tires had been slashed? I could have driven there…"

"Iian, I didn't call you because a tow truck was less than two minutes away. I'm used to taking care of myself. I've been doing it a very long time."

He saw frustration in her eyes, couldn't she see what he thought of her. He was sure it was written all over his face. His whole family knew what he thought of Allison Adams. Could he have been so stupid as to not show her what she meant to him?

"Ally, I care about you. We've known each other forever. I don't want anything bad to happen to you. I want to know everything that's going on with you. To be there when you get a call to go to Paris. Or when your mother needs help. When your tires are slashed." He leaned his forehead against hers. "I care too much," he whispered.

She had plenty of time to pull away. He made sure to give her that chance. Holding, hovering just a breath away from her, he made it her decision. He felt her vibrating, felt the shivers running through her body.

Looking into her face, he could see her decision written in her eyes. Then she was in his arms and kissing him. The taste of her filled his nose, his lips, intoxicating him beyond reason.

"Please," he said, against her lips. "Please let me stay."

Nodding her head as an answer, she pulled his mouth back to hers quickly. Not wanting to lose a moment, he pulled her closer, enjoying the softness of her. She was on her toes and just couldn't get close enough to him. So he pulled her up into his arms and carried her into her room, placing her down gently on the bed. Her hair was fanned out on the comforter, her eyes were clouded, and when she reached up for him, he swooped in to take her mouth with his again.

She was pulling on his pants trying to get them off of his hips as he was trying to remove her shirt. Their elbows hit and they looked at each other and laughed.

"Hurry," she said. He dragged her shirt over her head, then removed his own faster as she ran her hands over his chest.

He looked into her eyes as she said, "I love your chest, your arms, your body. I love the feel of you inside me."

When he kicked off his shoes and yanked his pants down, his erection sprang free.

"Oh, God, Iian! Be inside me." Her head fell back as he pulled her skirt up and pushed her newly purchased silk panties aside and placed his mouth to her heat. Her back came off the mattress, her hands went to his hair, holding or pushing, he didn't care.

Her scent was intoxicating. His tongue lapped at her until she bucked and pulled at him.

Then in one smooth motion, he pulled the silk down her legs and was inside her. He could feel her muscles contract around him and thought he would go blind. How could he be addicted to her so fast? The scents and feel of her were like a drug. His arms shook as he held himself over her, not wanting to move for fear that he'd embarrass himself and come entirely too soon. When he looked down into her eyes, he saw the desire and something else in them. Then she moved her hips and all thought left him.

Her nails dug into his shoulders, she bit her bottom lip on a moan. She was sure she'd screamed when he'd set his mouth to her. She knew she was screaming his name over and over as he pounded into her soft flesh. She wrapped her legs around his hips and held on. She enjoyed watching his face, set in concentration. Wanting to break that concentration, she reached up and pulled his mouth down to hers and licked his bottom lip. He moaned and picked up the pace to thrust deeper.

When he pulled her hips up and grabbed one of her legs, he held it close to his side which caused a new sensation that spread throughout her core. She was building too fast, she wanted to wait for him. Throwing her head back on a scream, she just couldn't wait any longer.

She was exquisite during an orgasm. Her face flushed, her skin glowed, and the smell of her was exquisite. When every bone in her body was relaxed, he flipped her over and proceeded to run his mouth down her lush bottom.

She may be tall and skinny, but her bottom was just ripe enough that he wanted a taste. Nibbling, he took his time and enjoyed her backside. When he saw her hips moving against his hands, he pulled her up onto her knees and entered her slowly from behind. He enjoyed the arch in her back as she twisted and writhed in front of him.

Leaning over, he whispered in her ear. "I love being inside you, Ally, I want to bury myself and never leave." He felt her body vibrate and knew she was moaning. "God, I wish I could hear all those sexy noises you make when I'm inside you." He continued to pump into her and felt her bodybuilding much like he was.

Her hips kept rotating as he pounded in her, and just before he lost control, he said, "Come with me, Ally."

He lay there until his heart slowed down. He could feel that she was totally relaxed next to him. He'd pulled her into the crook of his arm and enjoyed her soft bottom against his thighs.

When his mind settled he realized a few things; first, the bed was way too small for him. Second, he liked the new underwear she'd bought. Third, he wanted her again. Knowing she was completely relaxed and most likely asleep, he looked around the dark room. Here, he could see that she'd personalized a little. Her art supplies sat in the small corner, almost forgotten. She had a small jewelry case on the chest of drawers. The family picture Lacey had given her sat on her nightstand.

Then his stomach growled. Removing himself from the small bed, he pulled on his jeans and walked into the small kitchen. She hadn't moved, and he wondered if he could cook quietly enough without waking her. He didn't think he was a loud person; he tried not to bang the pans and dishes around when he cooked. To tell the truth, his family and co-workers had never told him if he was ever loud.

Looking into her fridge, he shook his head. How did she survive on next to nothing? Taking out a carton of eggs, he was pleased to see that it was not only full but fresh. He found an onion and some salsa in the back of the fridge. Finding a large skillet in the cupboard, he got to work making his first dinner for her.

Allison surfaced when Iian left the room. She'd been numb all over and her eyesight and hearing had just returned. How could she have gone this long without having sex that good? Her whole body vibrated. She was sure that if she tried to stand, her legs would just melt. She heard him moving around in the kitchen area and realized she hadn't even eaten lunch that day. Giving herself a few more minutes she rolled over and put herself back together before walking into the next room.

Whatever he was making smelled like heaven. She entered the room and her mouth watered. It wasn't just the food that had caused this. It was the sight of Iian standing in her kitchen, bare-chested, barefoot, with his faded jeans unbuckled and hanging low on his hips as he cooked. Walking into the room, she realized she was starving for him as well as hungry for food.

They sat out on the deck in the cool night air and ate omelets. She wondered how he could make simple eggs and some salsa taste so good.

He asked about her trip to visit her mother. When she voiced her concerns about her feeling guilty about putting her mother in a home, he jumped in.

"You're not trained to take care of someone with Alzheimer's. Ally, I did some research after your mother was diagnosed. Some of the things that people do when they have this disease can be confusing and hurtful. Most of the people end up walking around in a confused state and getting lost." He looked concerned. "What would you have done if your mother wandered off here," he motioned to the beach. "She could have gotten stuck in the bluff at high tide or lost in the woods."

Allison hadn't thought of that. Biting her bottom lip, she saw the truth in his words.

"I know the people at the Hotel are more equipped to deal with this disease. You can't think of yourself and how you think your mother would feel. Is your mother happy when you visit her?"

"Yes, she appears to be happy and healthy."

"Then focus on that. They are keeping her safe. Because you've taken this step, you may have very well saved her life. You did save her life already. Let her be happy there. Enjoy your visits and let her think she is on some extended vacation you've claimed she thinks she is on."

Pulling her close, he kissed her nose. "Don't worry if you have done the right thing. Just know that you've done the best thing for her."

Later, they lay in the small bed holding each other after making love slowly. She listened to the evening spring rain hit the roof. Closing her eyes, she wished that she could always feel this wanted. She listened to the rhythm of his heart and slid into sleep dreaming of him.

CHAPTER 15

*T*he next morning, shortly after Iian had left the cabin, she received a call from Ric. There was an art show this weekend in San Diego and some of her pieces were going to be highlighted. He wanted her to fly down and make an appearance.

He'd already gotten her a hotel room and her flight from Portland was booked. Ric wasn't one to take no for an answer. She decided to stop by the Golden Oar after work and see if Iian wanted to spend the weekend with her in California.

She'd had so much fun teaching the children that day, that she was on an emotional high when she walked into the Golden Oar later. Then she stopped dead in her tracks after she'd entered the front doors.

Iian stood next to the bar and Lori Roberts was wrapped around him like a second skin. His back was to the door, but when she'd walked in, his head snapped around and his eyes zoned in on her.

Taking a big breath, she walked right up to him and

slapped him across the face, hard. Not waiting for a response, she marched out the door without a word. Her eyes stung by the time she reached for her car door. Just as she was opening it, she was spun around.

"I wasn't doing anything with Lori, I was trying to get her to leave in the taxi there," he pointed to the white cab that she'd just walked around.

Looking over she noticed one of his staff members was pouring the very drunk woman into the cab.

Allison laughed.

"God, I'm so stupid." She looked over at him and noticed the red mark on his cheek. "Oh my God! Iian, I am so sorry!" She grabbed his face and examined his cheek.

He was laughing at this point. He pulled her into a big hug and started kissing her right there in the parking lot.

"You can slap me anytime you want, I didn't feel anything. If you were ever that mad at me again, I think it would break me. When I saw you leave…" He put his forehead to hers. "Don't leave me again. I don't want to be with anyone else Ally. Just you, move in with me, I want you close to me."

She jerked back and looked into his face. Tears were coming to her eyes now and she smiled up at him and nodded her head.

"Tonight?" He asked eagerly for her answer.

"Yes, Iian. I'll move in with you tonight." He kissed her again.

"Good, I have a few things I have to finish up here first." He grabbed a ring of keys from his pocket. "Here, this one is for the front door." He removed a key from the circle. "You grab a few things and head over, then we can take tomorrow and get the rest of your stuff." He pulled her into another embrace and spun her around in a circle, laughing.

~

She felt like she was still spinning when she parked her car in front of Megan's. Megan was sitting on the front porch where the children were playing quietly next to her. Taking a deep breath, she walked over to her friend and told her the news.

"Finally!" Megan had said and given her a large hug.

Did everyone in town know that they were sleeping together? If they didn't, that little display at the Golden Oar should assure them that they were now a couple. Moving in with Iian was a large step. She'd never lived with anyone before.

Sure, she had plenty of boyfriends, but she'd never gotten close enough to them to feel comfortable to actually live with them. She knew Iian was different.

As she walked to her cabin a while later to gather some of her belongings, she thought about him.

She wanted to be with him, she wanted to wake up with him beside her. She liked his sense of humor, the way he looked at ease with everything he did. The way he carried himself and the way he was with his nephew and niece. He would be a great father; she could just imagine their children.

She stopped in the middle of the path and blinked a few times. What was she doing? She was thinking of having children with Iian! Was she in love with him? She didn't know. She'd felt something for him for as long as she could remember. But was it love? She continued on the path and when she reached the cabin, she was so caught up in her thoughts that she almost stepped on it.

There on the front porch, just outside her front door. It was larger this time. Maybe a cat or a raccoon? Its skin had been meticulously removed. Blood pooled around the small form this time its head had been removed as well. Looking up, she saw that it had been speared with a large narrow stick that had been thrust through the animal's mouth into the wood of the front door. The door's bright red was a complete contrast from the darker red of the bloody skinned head. The words "Die Bitch" were written on the door with the blood.

Stepping back, she quickly looked around. Pulling out her new cell phone from her pocket, she punched a few buttons and sent her text.

"Don't touch anything! I'm on my way. So is Robert. Go to Megan's, she's expecting you.

She met Megan halfway down the path. She had a large wooden bat in her hand and her cell phone in the other. "I've got her," she said to no one.

Then Allison realized that Megan was on speaker phone with Todd, when he said, "Good, get your butts back to the house and sit tight. We're on our way."

"Where are the kids?" Allison asked, trying to control the shaking.

"Lacey showed up right after you left. She's got them on lockdown in the house. Are you okay, sweetie?" Her friend asked her as she pulled her along the path quickly.

"I… I thought it was like last time. But this time it was deliberate."

"Last time? Did this happen to you before?"

"At the house, before the fire. I thought it was an animal that had done it."

Finally, they reached the house. Lacey opened the door when she saw her friend approach, her large stomach protruding in front of her small frame.

"Are you alright, Allison?" She gathered her friend close.

They had no more than shut the door when Iian and Todd drove up. Both men jumped from the car and sprinted to the front door. Lacey opened it and stepped out.

"We're alright. Everyone is okay." She stepped back as Iian rushed in to grab Allison. Todd did the same to his wife and grabbed both his kids in a family hug, all over the cheers from his kids of "Daddy, Daddy."

Just before Robert showed up, Aaron drove up and the scene was repeated for Lacey.

Aaron didn't want Lacey to remain there. He complained about how close she was to her due date and tried to get her to go home, but in the end, friendship won over pregnancy. Allison did notice that they had agreed she could stay if she remained in the study with her feet up.

So, when Robert showed up, Allison stepped out onto the front porch and repeated her story.

When she reached the end, the three men, leaving Aaron behind with the women, walked out to the cabin to see the damage.

An hour later, Iian walked Allison to her car. He'd gathered some of her things in her overnight bag and they drove in silence to his place.

He cooked a wonderful meal of caramelized salmon and wild rice with fresh vegetables. She could get used to eating like this. It wasn't just the food that impressed her, but when he cooked it was like watching a dance. He was so fluent in the kitchen that she doubted he knew how graceful he was. His tall frame fit right in and he appeared to melt into the motions.

She'd tried to help him and ended up just in his way. So, she'd sat back at the bar on a tall stool, drinking a glass of wine and watched the show. There was just something so sexy about Iian cooking in the kitchen.

Not until they were laying in the large bed, their breaths coming quickly from the marathon of great sex they'd just had, did she finally sit up and ask him.

"Does Robert think it was Kevin?" He sat up and pulled her close.

"Yes, he was heading over there to ask him questions." He tried to hold her still so the conversation was over, but she pulled free from his arms.

"Iian, I want to know what you think. Do you think Kevin would do something like this? I know he's had a problem with drinking, but the Kevin we knew in high school would never hit his children, never threaten someone with dead animals." Then she remembered the day in the parking lot, everything he'd said to her and she shivered.

"Allison, you've been gone a few years. Right after you left, the bank foreclosed on his house. Then his father died and left him with a large pile of debt." His eyes grew darker. "He turned to drinking almost immediately. He stopped being the model citizen shortly after and became the town bully and drunk. Actually, he always was a bully, just not a vicious one like he is now."

"I just don't want to believe he would cross that line." She allowed him to pull her down next to him.

"I can. I've had to deal with him a few times and he's changed. No more talk about this tonight. We'll go and get the rest of your stuff tomorrow. Todd was cleaning up the mess outside, so you won't have to see that again. Let's get some sleep." He kissed the top of her head and she snuggled down next to him. It was many hours later that she finally fell asleep.

The next day she stood on the front porch of the cabin. If she hadn't seen it herself the day before, she would have never guessed that there had been a bloody mess.

As she gathered up her new items in the living room, she thought about the fire. About her tires. About all the other things that had been going on to her.

Iian walked into the room from the back with a bag full of her new undergarments and a large goofy smile on his face.

"I didn't know it was my birthday," he smiled and set everything down in the suitcase he'd brought for her clothes.

Laughing she said, "I did buy you something special. If you're good, I might just show you later tonight."

"Woohoo!" He shouted and turned to gather the rest of her items from the back room like a kid in a candy store.

When they arrived back at the house, Robert was there waiting by his car.

"Evening," he said, as they stepped out of the car. "If you have a few minutes, I'd like to talk to you both."

"Sure, come on in." They settled in the living room.

"Well, the bad news is, Kevin wasn't at his place. We talked to his wife and she hasn't seen him for several weeks. She thinks he went hunting shortly after she left him. I've got everyone out looking for him. We're checking everywhere he usually goes. He has a cabin up on Gunner Hill, but it was empty and looked like he hadn't been there for a while."

"What about the tires and the fire?" Iian asked.

"We don't have any proof that he was in Edgeview. Or that he started the fire that night. All we know is that we can't account for him after you saw him at the park."

"So basically, you haven't figured anything else out yet." Iian stood and started pacing.

Later, after Robert left and as Iian cooked them dinner, she asked him about the trip to California.

"Ric called me the other day and asked me to go to San Diego for an art show this next weekend. Some of my art is going to be featured and I was wondering if you would like to go with me."

She held her breath waiting for his reply.

He took his time replying. "Are you driving down there?"

"No, I'll be flying."

"I've never flown before," he signed back. "I'd love to go to your art show." He walked over and kissed her lightly. "It'll be nice to get out of town for the weekend."

They sat and ate dinner in the living room while watching a movie. She could tell Iian got frustrated halfway through it, trying to read the subtitles, so she grabbed the remote and switched it to a ball game. He smiled, and they sat back and enjoyed the game together.

Two hours later he lay with Allison wrapped around him, the little see-through black lace she'd purchased just for him was somewhere on the floor. Seeing her in it had totally destroyed him.

He lay there feeling her steady breath on his shoulder and felt confident that he was armed with a plan. First thing in the morning he would start messaging his brother and brother-in-law. For the next few days, at least until they left for California, he'd make sure Allison wouldn't be left alone.

The next morning, after his messages and making plans with his family, he'd jumped in the shower with her, but this time his mind was on getting clean and getting dressed. She'd tried several times to start something, but he was having none of it.

Tossing a large towel in her direction, he said, "Wrap this around yourself and come with me." He grabbed a towel himself and hastily tied it around his hips. He didn't even wait to see a response from her.

Walking down the hall, he looked over his shoulder in time to see her grab a terry robe from one of her bags.

He led her down the hallway where he'd placed a green ribbon on the doorknob. He nodded for her to open it. He'd meant to show her what he'd made for her last night, but they'd been so busy it had been the last thing on his mind.

Now he watched her as she opened the door and pushed it wide. He saw the expression on her face go from confusion to excitement so quickly. Then she was running into the room looking around with complete and utter awe.

He could tell she was saying something, but she was running around touching everything, looking in every direction that he couldn't see what she was saying. He sat back and watched her with a large smile on his face.

～

The room was more than she'd ever dreamed of. He had everything. There was a large easel in front of the huge bay windows. Canvases of every size leaned against one wall there was a desk full of paints and brushes of every variety. Some of them looked very old, but still in great condition.

Then she saw the drafting table. She walked over to it and ran her fingers along its aged wood. Everything she could ever hope for was here in this large room. Turning, she saw Iian standing in the doorway with the towel wrapped loosely around his hips. His arms were crossed over his chest.

"You did this all for me?"

"No, I'm thinking of taking up painting." He smiled and walked towards her.

"Iian, I don't know what to say."

"You don't have to say anything. Some of these were my grandmother's. I think she would be happy that they went to you instead of sitting in the attic collecting dust. I hope I didn't miss anything. Lacey and Megan helped me pick out most of this stuff." He walked over and toyed with a pen knife used to cut canvases.

He turned back to her in time to see her wipe a tear from her cheek.

"Oh no!" he walked over to her, "My sisters assured me that this was a *no crying gift*."

She laughed.

"I know everyone else in town gave you items to help replace what you lost. I wanted to do something for you as well."

"Iian, it's perfect. Thank you." She took his face in her hands and kissed him.

"Mmmm, how about finishing that shower? I think I see a few spots we missed." He started to pull her robe off her shoulders causing her to laugh again.

The rest of the week passed quickly. Allison had started painting in her new studio. She enjoyed the brightness of the room and the wonderful view out the large windows. She'd changed a few things around, moving the drafting table to the other wall with Iian's help. She thought that it made the room flow better. Iian agreed.

She would spend a few hours up there every evening until Iian arrived home.

When she visited her mother in Edgeview, Iian had come along for the ride.

For some reason, over the last week, she felt like she was never left alone in the house by herself for too long. Someone was always over there for one reason or the other when Iian was at work.

Once, Megan and the kids had come over for a visit. She always had paper and colors for the kids to draw on and keep them entertained while they chatted.

Lacey came over and Allison forced her to sit in the living room with her feet up. They had watched an old movie, and Lacey had fallen asleep on the couch until her husband had come to take her home.

Once, Todd even came over and said he needed to use their home gym. She had gone up to her art room and worked while he worked out. An hour later, she had wanted a snack. When she went downstairs, she found him sitting on the couch in the living room watching a ball game.

That's when she knew that everyone was watching out for her, and she knew it was all Iian's doing.

How could she be mad at him for having his family watch out for her? She loved them even more for it.

Iian had a busy week before their weekend trip to California. He trusted his staff to take care of the place for the weekend, so that wasn't a major concern.

He'd been rushing around the place, getting it ready for the Elks club annual dinner that night, when Lori and Jenny walked in. It appeared that they were having another "girls night out". Not wanting to be stuck in the middle of that mess, he tried to escape to the back with no luck. Why did it seem the women had tentacles instead of hands when it came to touching him?

He couldn't keep them from grabbing or pinching him, it really was becoming annoying. Finally, after pulling them to a more private area, he had firmly told them that he was involved with someone and was no longer on the "play" list.

Both women had looked at him as if he had physically dealt them a blow. The end result pleased him, as they stormed out of the doors and left him to finish setting the dining room up.

He thought of Allison, waiting at home for him, and smiled. How could he ever go back home and not expect her to be there waiting for him? He'd even started thinking of the old place as theirs, instead of his family's. He now thought of his dad's room as their room instead. She'd completed the place, she made it into a home.

hen the small plane had taken off, Iian had a quick moment of sheer terror. Then Allison had grabbed his hand and he'd focused on looking at her fingers wrapped in his. Slowly he started to relax so that by the time they had landed, he'd felt totally at ease and even a little eager to fly again.

When they reached the hotel, they had less than an hour until they were to be at the art show. He could see the tension building in her and tried to keep her calm, so she could enjoy the evening. After she walked out of the bathroom in the little red dress, all he could think about was how to keep her in the room and all to himself.

When she had walked out of the bathroom, Iian gave her the strangest look. First, she thought she'd gotten something on her dress. Then she thought he didn't like the dress.

He stood across the room in his dark suit. She couldn't remember the last time she'd seen him dress up. He was handsome in jeans and a t-shirt, but in a suit, he was a knock-out. His hair was slicked back to curl around his neck. His tie matched the silver in his eyes, eyes which were raking her up and down.

"Are you sure we have to go to this thing tonight? We could just stay here," he signed as he started to walk across the room to her.

"Oh no!" She held up her hands to ward him off. Then she signed, "I didn't get dressed up to stay in this hotel room. Plus, I'm starving."

He grabbed her outstretched hands and took them to his lips, placing a soft kiss on both of them. Then he looked up at her and said, "You look beautiful. Let's make it a short night, I want to get you back here and out of that dress as soon as possible."

She felt the pull deep inside; she wanted that too. Shaking her head in agreement, she moistened her lips against the hunger she felt for him.

Ric Derby stood amongst the crowd of his people and knew the second his favorite artist walked in the door. Not only did the room fall almost silent, but the little red number she wore screamed, "*look at me!*"

In the two years, he'd know Allison Adams, their relationship had grown to a brother-sister caliber. He'd never had this close of a relationship with any other artists before. It was probably due to the easy nature of Allison. Most artists he worked with were tortured souls. Ally was different. Wherever she went, sunshine was there. Her art truly reflected what was in her soul. Pureness.

Smiling, he handed an empty flute of champagne to a waiter and walked over to greet her. He could feel the eyes of the whole room watch as he walked up and placed a soft kiss on her cheek.

"You look wonderful tonight, Ally. I'm so glad you could come," he whispered in her ear.

Pulling back, he then noticed the man standing next to her. He'd met Iian Jordan on several occasions. The brother to Todd Jordan, whom he had been doing business with for many years, a man Ric truly admired and respected. Todd was the husband to Megan, a woman Ric admired and respected even more.

Stretching his hand out to shake Iian's he remembered that Iian was deaf. Having learned sign language after he'd worked on a project with a deaf artist group several years back, he extended a welcome.

"Hello Iian, it's good to see you again. I'm sorry I'm a little rusty with sign language, I hope you'll overlook any mistakes. Please, come in, would you like anything to drink?"

Twenty minutes later, Ric watched as Iian and Allison wandered the room. He liked seeing Ally's eyes light up when Iian would sign or say something to her. He noticed that Iian didn't speak to anyone else but would lean close to Ally and whisper something to her. He enjoyed watching the couple browse the room and felt an over-whelming sense of jealousy and loneliness sink in.

~

Iian watched as Allison melted into the crowd effortlessly. He looked around and realized this was where she belonged. Here amongst the high rollers who wore diamonds as easily as he wore a chef toque and uniform.

He looked across the room and saw Ric Derby, who was watching Allison with an eagle eye. Iian had a little moment of jealousy there when he'd seen the man greet her at the door. The light kiss he had given her had caused some alarm, but then he remembered the New Year's party Allison and Ric had attended together. Iian had kissed Ally that night and he knew they were just friends. Which didn't ease the tension he tried to avoid when the man looked at her.

He turned and watched her talking to an older couple. He stood back almost in the shadows and just watched the crowd.

Then there was a light hand on his arm. Turning, he saw a woman with long blonde hair and the tightest dress he'd had the pleasure of experiencing. She was trying to talk to him, but he just wasn't catching anything she was saying. She leaned forward, and he could smell her soft breath on his face. He tried to take a step back but realized he was up against the wall.

She continued to talk to him and started to put her body against his. He almost panicked.

"I'm sorry," he started to say. Then he felt another hand on his shoulder and the woman backed up a few steps. Turning, he saw Ric standing to his side.

Ric signed to him, "Iian, this is Countess Regina. She is from Sweden. I've told her that you're deaf. She would like to know what your thoughts are of this particular piece. She is in the market to purchase it, but is unsure and would like a man's opinion since she will be buying it for her husband."

Iian turned and looked at the art in question. It was one of Allison's pieces. The large canvas hosted a colorful scene of the waters off the shore of Pride, a white sailboat floated in the distance. Stepping closer he could see a storm brewing in the distance. Then he looked closer at the boat. *"Dawn-treader"* was etched on the side.

An image flashed in his mind of his father standing at the helm. It was so strong it almost knocked him back. Taking a breath, he looked closer at the image before him. He could make out two forms on the boat. One at the helm and one manning the ropes at the front.

Closing his eyes on the pain, he steadied himself.

Then something else took over his thoughts. It wasn't pain, but a calmness that started to spread through him. Opening his eyes, he looked at the piece with renewed interest.

Turning, he looked past the blonde woman and Ric.

Allison stood there watching him. Her eyes riveted to his.

He said, loud and clear. "It's the most heart-warming thing I've seen in ten years. It brings to mind a life journey on calm and rough seas. Of loneliness, sorrow, and the joy of returning home. Any man would be honored to have such a wonderful piece of work hanging in his home." He turned to the countess and realized that the woman was close to tears.

She said something else that with her accent he was unable to understand. He looked to Ric to see what was said.

"That was beautiful. You have a way of expressing the

unseen. Thank you for your wonderful words. My husband thanks you for his new piece of art," Ric translated.

Ric smiled at Iian and then turned and took the countess and walked with her to complete the transaction.

"Well, I hope you're happy. I've just sold this piece to a countess, no less," he signed to Allison when she walked up to him.

"I'm happy because you realized what it's about. It's not about the horrors that happened that day to you, but the joy of you coming home." She stepped into his arms and said, "Iian, I'm so glad that you came home." Then she kissed him right there, in front of her masterpiece.

"I want you. Now! Tell me we can get out of here," he said against her lips.

She nodded her head. "Let me make my excuses. I'll be just a moment." She kissed him again and walked away.

He watched her go and felt something shift inside him. Looking back at the canvas, he walked closer and took another look. There in the bottom right corner was Allison's signature with a date scribbled underneath. She'd painted this the same year he'd lost his hearing. He looked up at it again with renewed wonder. A seventeen-year-old Allison had painted something a countess from Sweden had just paid high six digits for.

He'd seen her other art and he liked the fairies and other creatures she'd painted. A lot of it had reminded him of his grandmother's stuff that still hung on the walls of the Golden Oar. Making up his mind, he walked over to were Ric stood, still talking to the countess.

When Allison walked up to him a few minutes later, he was back in front of her painting smiling like he had a secret.

By the time they entered the lobby of the hotel, he couldn't keep his hands off her. The dress stretched tight over her curves and he watched as her hips swayed with each step.

When the elevator doors closed, he pulled her into his arms and kissed her. He ran his hands up and down her sides, then stopped and leaned back.

"Just what do you have on underneath this thing?" He asked.

She gave him a wicked smile and mouthed "Nothing."

He couldn't remember getting into their room. He thought he fumbled with the door and at one point cursed the damn credit card key locks.

Then they were inside and he was inside her against the back of the door. His hands fisted in her hair, and he pulled her head back to expose her neck as he ran his mouth over the long curve.

She tasted like the sun, hot and ripe for him. He could feel her vibrate with every moan of pleasure. His dress pants had pooled at his feet, so when he tried to move he'd almost ended up on his ass.

She laughed and held on to him as he thrust deeper and harder. He could tell the differences in her body. How could he not notice when her skin started to glow right before she was about to come? She vibrated with every moment of pleasure he gave her and when she peaked, he felt her convulse on him, and then he released himself to the pleasure as well.

Allison was glad to be back in Pride. She'd enjoyed the

short trip with Iian, they'd ended up spending most of their time in the hotel room. They did take a break and go to one of his friend's restaurants downtown. The Italian place was fancy, and the food was even fancier. Not that she was complaining, she just liked the hometown feeling the Golden Oar provided more than the upscale variety.

Iian had spoken to his friend for a while. The man had even sat at their table and talked to them in sign language. It was nice to know that he had other friends out there. She had gotten nervous when the man had hinted that Iian should move his restaurant to San Diego since he would make a better living in a larger city. Iian just shook his head and said that he was already making a good living in Pride.

There was something about coming home to the big house with Iian that felt right. She spent the first half of her Monday in her new art room. She'd cried at the loss of the three paintings that had burned in the fire. They were the first pieces she'd done in almost a year that truly had more meaning to her than most of the others.

So, she sat back down and started re-creating one of her favorites that had burned up. It had taken her almost a week to finish it the first time. This time she knew exactly what she wanted and thought it would take her half the time.

She enjoyed teaching and was thankful that she had three days during the week that she could still have to herself. Part-time was perfect for her schedule. Knowing summer was coming up, she looked forward to having more time since she'd only agreed to teach at the boys and girls club for two days a week.

She needed the extra time for her art and her mother.

The short fifteen-minute drive to Edgeview always felt like a relaxing trip. The winding roads were wide, and the scenery was always breathtaking, no matter the season. She'd found a few places she wanted to stop and paint. Knowing this summer, she would have that chance, she made mental notes on them.

She'd found out that the best time to visit her mother was after four o'clock. That way, lunch was out of the way and it was still too early for the evening Bingo session, which was after dinner at six.

Her mother seemed to enjoy every visit and she actually looked like she was enjoying herself at the Hotel. She kept talking like it was all some elaborate vacation. She didn't want to discourage that thinking.

Megan had gone with her one day and taken a picture of them out on the balcony with the sun setting behind them. She'd blow up two copies and had framed them, one for herself and the other, she'd hung on her mother's wall. It felt good to have another picture to keep as a treasure.

Today her mother hadn't been in such a good mood. She was complaining about the lunch they'd had. She kept saying over and over that it was Tuesday and she wanted the salmon instead of the lemon pepper chicken.

When Allison tried to explain to her that it was indeed Monday, her mother looked her right in the eye and said, "Of course I know it's Tuesday. You know you remind me of my daughter Allison. Have you met her? She was just here." Then she looked around the room as if she was trying to find her. She'd left the Hotel with a heavy heart.

She'd done her shopping at Walmart slowly. Her mind kept racing over questions. Would there be a day soon, when her mother didn't recognize her at all? Since moving her to the Hotel, she'd noticed that her mother had ingrained herself so deeply into the people there that she appeared so happy. Was that a good thing? Or was it causing a larger rift between mother and daughter that would completely close in time due to Alzheimer's?

Driving home, Allison played that scene over and over in her head. She watched as the sun sunk lower on the horizon. The peaceful drive became a burden and she just wished she was home with Iian.

Then bright lights came out of no-where. A large truck with its high beams on rushed up so close to her bumper she thought it was going to hit her. Her heart began to race. The lights blinded her until she reached over and flipped her rear-view mirror down to night mode, which helped shield most of the brightness. Still, her side mirrors reflected the bright lights directly into her eyes. When she thought the truck was going to back off, it flipped on two searchlights that were mounted on top of a roll bar. These lights were so bright, Allison swerved to stay on the road. Grasping her steering wheel, she did everything she could to stay within the lines.

She thought about grabbing her cell phone, but it was still in her purse on the floor of the passenger side. Concentrating on maintaining her speed, she was totally unprepared when the truck bumped her car from behind. It wasn't hard, just a tap, but her wheels turned with the momentum and she had to yank her wheel back before she ran off the side of the road. Just as she got her tires back on the road and out of the gravel, she was hit again, this time a lot harder. She screamed as her hands grasped tighter to the wheel. Her head bobbed back and forth with the motion. Her neck screamed at the tension.

Trying to think if there was a turnoff ahead, she watched with fear as the truck backed off and prepared to ram her again.

Then she saw her chance. Up ahead was a small turn off. If she could fake like she was going to pull off, she might be able to gain enough speed to outrun the truck.

As it approached, she gassed her tiny Honda praying that the small engine would have enough in it to outrun the larger vehicle. Just before the turnoff, she yanked on her wheel hard to the right. The truck was so close that when it pulled to the right, its tires caused the gravel to spit up past the windows. Waiting until the last second, she yanked her wheel to the left just in time to avoid a large cement barrier.

The truck had been going too fast to make the turn. She watched in horror as it slammed on its brakes. She could hear the tires on the gravel. Reaching down, she yanked her purse into her lap and frantically reached for her cell phone.

Knowing she couldn't text since she was focused on watching her rear-view mirror, she dialed the next person who came to mind.

Less than two minutes later, she passed the Pride's welcome sign with no sight of the truck behind her. Two more minutes and she saw Todd's jeep coming towards her. He passed her and turned around and followed her to Four Corners, a small local gas station.

When her car stopped, she just sat there as Todd approached her window. Her hands were glued to the steering wheel, her phone was sitting on her lap, and she realized she was still on speaker phone with Megan.

"Todd's here. I'm okay. We're at Four Corners. Thank you so much, Megan."

"I'm glad you're okay. Iian and Robert are on their way. I'll talk to you later."

She removed her fingers one at a time from the steering wheel and noticed how white her knuckles were just as Todd knocked on her window.

"Are you okay?" he asked, opening her door.

"I'm fine, I'm just shaken up," she climbed out of her car and her legs felt wobbly. She looked up as she heard Iian's motorcycle fly down the road towards them. Robert's cruiser was not far behind him.

Iian had jumped off the bike and quickly gathered her in his arms.

"Damn it, Todd, tell that brother of yours that I don't care who's in danger, he can't do eighty on that damn bike through town," Robert said as he got out of his car.

Allison and Todd laughed.

"Are you okay Allison?" Robert asked as he approached.

Pulling out of Iian's death grip, she signed along. "Yes, I'm fine. Just a little shaken up, I think." She looked at Robert and answered the question that was on everyone's mind. "It was Kevin's truck, but I couldn't see if he was behind the wheel."

"Damn it!" She heard Iian cuss for the first time. He pulled his hands through his hair and started to pace.

"Let's just have a look at your car." Robert walked to the back of her Honda. Everyone followed him.

She'd lost her back bumper in the last hit. Both of her brake lights were gone. Her trunk had been flung open and she was sure the latch was history.

"Did a number on the car. Are you sure you're okay? No head or back pain?" Robert asked as he took out his pad to write something down.

"No, I had my seatbelt on. I didn't hit my head or anything. I think I'm just shaken up." She rubbed her neck and was thankful.

Iian came to stand in front of her. He quickly asked her the same questions Robert had. She took her time and answered him.

"I'm going to have to tow your car in. It'll be at Rusty's shop. I'm sure you'll want him to fix it up, anyway. This way, I can take pictures and whatever else we need for evidence." Robert bent and pulled a twisted piece of metal that had lodged in between two corners of her jagged car. "Well, it appears I have all the evidence I need right here." he turned the metal around to show everyone an Oregon license plate that was not her own and no doubt belonged on Kevin's truck.

Iian was feeling restless. He sat on the large bed waiting for Allison to get out of the shower. Todd had driven her home in the Jeep with him right behind them on his bike. He should have taken the day off and driven with her to Edgeview. What if she had died? He knew the road to Edgeview. There were lots of twist and turns, and most of all, there were places where the guardrail was the only thing protecting a car from plummeting off a cliff to a watery grave.

Damn it! He stood up and started to pace again. He couldn't stand to live without her. She'd only been living in the house for a little over a week, but already the place was less empty with her there. She didn't have a lot of stuff; in fact, she'd only brought what she had been given by the town's people. But it was the small things that she did to make it feel different.

He looked at the small vase of flowers she'd placed on the table next to the large screen television. He opened a drawer and saw it full of her night things. He could smell her in every part of the house. Her wonderful scent drifted around the place like it had always been there.

Walking down the hall, he stepped into her studio and smiled. There on one of the easels was what he could only describe as a self-portrait. Stepping closer he realized it wasn't Allison that looked back at him, but the face of her mother. The younger version of the woman was standing in front of an outline of a lighthouse, alone. The isolation of the lone figure didn't escape his eye. Everything was still in pencil, but he could see the beauty of the art and could imagine the colors she would use to finish the piece.

He felt the floor vibrate and looked over his shoulder as Allison walked in smiling.

"There you are. Is everything okay?" She approached him. She wore a soft pink silk robe tied with a colorful tie around her waist. Her hair was wet and flowing around her face in tresses.

"I was just thinking. It's a lovely piece. Your Mother?" he questioned.

"Yes, I'm going to donate the proceeds to the National Alzheimer Project. I have a few others that will be included," she walked over and looked at the drawing. "The original burned," she signed without looking at him.

He pulled her into his arms. "I want to show you something. Can you meet me for lunch tomorrow at the restaurant?"

She pulled back and looked at him. He held himself still.

"Yes, I can be there around noon. Is that okay?"

"It's perfect." He pulled her back to him and held on.

Iian had left early in the morning, so early in fact that Allison was still in bed when he'd snuck out of it.

She wouldn't have gotten up in time if it hadn't been for her alarm going off, something she hadn't had to set since living with him. It seemed that he always woke up at a quarter to six. She supposed it was some sort of internal clock.

She'd dressed quickly and tied her hair in a bun on the top of her head. Rushing out the door, she almost forgot her portfolio and had to race through the early morning mist back into the house to get it. Driving Iian's car, she drove through town. She had something special she wanted to show the kids today. She'd worked on it for several hours since her trip.

When she had presented them with the large caricature drawing of the entire class, everyone gathered around it and laughed. She had pinned it on the bulletin board and enjoyed seeing everyone laugh about their own funny faces staring back at them.

When she walked into the Golden Oar for lunch, she'd been so preoccupied that she was inside the door before she realized the place was empty. Where was everyone?

She looked around and was tempted to walk into the back, someplace she'd yet to visit.

Then Iian walked out. He wore a dark suit and had a funny look on his face. He strolled across the floor towards her.

"Hi, Ally."

"Hi, where is everyone?" She started to fidget under his intense gaze.

"There's a private party booked for lunch. Follow me." At first, she thought he was going to lead her into the back room. Maybe they were going to have lunch back there due to the private party using the whole dining area.

But when they turned the corner and she saw the table set up, she realized *they* were the private party.

The room was cleared except for one table that sat between the fireplace and the large windows that over-looked the water. The table was set, and candles sparkled in the dimness of the room.

"I've made us a special lunch if you will take a seat." He pulled out the chair for her. She smiled as she took a seat.

Then he said, "I'll be right back."

She sat there and looked around, waiting for him to return. His grandmother's painting still hung over the fire-place. The mermaid sat eternally combing her hair. Allison smiled at it. She was the reason she'd started drawing and painting. Then she turned her head and noticed a large white sheet over another canvas. She couldn't remember what painting had been there. Why had they covered it? Standing up, she walked over and started to pull the sheet aside.

Then she gasped. It was the Dawn-treader. How had he

gotten her painting? She thought the countess from Sweden had purchased this painting. Turning, she watched Iian walk in with two plates expertly balanced in his hands.

Setting them down, he smiled at her. "I had hoped to unveil it myself." He walked over to her.

"How did you get this? I thought it sold."

"It did sell, just not to a countess. I convinced her to buy your other shoreline scene and purchased this one. It belongs here." He looked up at the boat. "He belongs here."

"Iian, I don't know what to say," she signed. "Thank you." She felt honored that her art hung across the wall from the piece that had started her on the path to a career. Especially this piece. She'd worked so hard as a seventeen-year-old girl, who had just lost her sister, to do something so meaningful.

She'd taken it from a memory she had of watching Iian and his father leave the docks that day ten years ago. She'd gone down there to wish him a happy birthday. Something she would have never had the courage to do, except that during a visit to Abby in the hospital, her sister had told her to grab what she wanted in life, because life was too short, and Abby just wanted her to be happy enough for both of them.

The first thing that had crossed her seventeen-year-old mind had been Iian.

So, foolishly she had rushed down to the restaurant, and Lacey had told her that her father was taking him out on the boat for his birthday. Taking a chance, she had rushed to the docks just in time to see them sail off. She had sat there at the end of the dock and cried. Not for the missed opportunity but cried for her sister and the love that she knew she'd never get to experience.

"This is all so wonderful Iian. I can't thank you enough."

"Ally," he waited until she turned to him. "Will you marry me?"

"What?" She looked into his eyes, dumbfounded.

"I don't want to wake up another morning without you. I don't want to go to sleep another night without you by my side. I close my eyes and I can smell you, I can see you everywhere I look. If I think hard enough, I can remember what your voice sounds like and when you talk, I hear you."

Tears had escaped her eyes and he gently wiped them away. Then he bent down and kissed her eyes one at a time.

"I've waited a long time for you. You're the only one I can imagine spending my life with. In our house, having children with, and growing old with. Please, Ally, marry me."

"Say it, Iian. Please." She looked into his face and waited for the words she'd wanted to hear for so long.

"I love you, Ally, please say yes."

"I love you too, Iian. Yes, I'll marry you…" She was spun around quickly and laughed as she held onto him.

"Did you know that I've had a fantasy playing in my head of you wearing an outfit just like this?"

She laughed again.

He looked down at her simple black skirt and white button up top. Then he reached up and pulled her hair loose from the bun, and when it spilled down, he moaned as the smile left her lips. Desire spilled into her so fast that when he backed her up against the wall, she felt a shiver race through her bones.

"Iian, we can't here…" She whispered.

"I sent everyone home until one. We can, and we will, right here," he pulled her skirt up exposing her soft flesh and the silky black lace that covered her. He watched her eyes fog over as he touched her gently.

"I want to be inside you so bad. I've wanted nothing else since I watched you walk in. I want to go slow, but…"

"No, please, I can't wait either. Please Iian," she moaned as his fingers entered her more quickly. She reached for his zipper just as he yanked the silky lace down her legs. She got one foot free as he plunged into her heat. His hands were on either side of her, bracing himself against the wall. She arched her back as he continued to pound relentlessly into her swollen flesh.

How could she want him this bad? She enjoyed the speed and grabbed his hips to force him to speed up even more. His long deep thrusts did little to soothe the desire she felt building. Then he grabbed one of her legs and brought it up beside him and she felt each thrust with a new sense of love. He was everything she'd ever desired, and he was taking her against the wall of a very public place, which made it even more exciting and dangerous.

Then she lost all ability to think as his fingers reached down between them and touched her small nub and she exploded around him just as he screamed in triumph.

CHAPTER 17

*S*he was late getting back to school and had less time to set up for her class that she'd wanted. Her shirt was wrinkled, and she couldn't stop smiling.

Since it was the last week of school, the kids were more hyper than usual.

The children had all sat there in their chairs fidgeting as she'd prepared her art project that they were going to do for the day. She was pleased to see Tommy back in her class. Tanya had assured her that the children were living with Brenda at her mother's house in town. Since they hadn't found Kevin yet, Brenda was picking the kids up herself, instead of having them ride the bus to and from the school.

Iian had changed his work schedule around so that he would be home for her after school. She was driving his car since her car was still at Rusty's getting the necessary repairs she hadn't complained.

They were planning on telling the family of their

engagement tonight during dinner at Megan's place. The evening couldn't come quick enough.

After their mind-blowing sex against the wall, he'd presented her with his mother's ring, which had been passed down from the family. It was a beautiful emerald in a simple silver setting. She couldn't have picked out anything more perfect. Looking at it on her finger gave her a sense of family. Iian's mother had died giving birth to him, so he'd never known her, but wearing her ring made her feel like she was part of something bigger.

Iian stood in the kitchen and just couldn't focus. He was too excited. The dinner crew had shown up less than half an hour after Allison had left. His body was still vibrating from the hot and fast sex he'd had in the dining room. He would never cross that room again without thinking of Allison against the wall dressed in the sexy teacher outfit from his dreams. Damn, he was getting hard again he had to stop thinking about his fiancée. He smiled to himself again.

Then he looked up as Lacey strolled in through the double doors. "Strolled" wasn't the right word. Waddled? He watched her make her way across the room and almost laughed at her.

"Don't you dare laugh at me!" she signed from across the floor.

"What are you doing here? I thought you were on house arrest after Aaron caught you shopping last week." He walked her back to his office. He knew he could force her to sit on the couch with her feet up if he could get her back there.

"I'm restless at home and I wanted some of your…" She didn't get any further. She hunched over and grabbed her stomach as a gush of fluid flooded the floor at her feet.

Iian freaked. He's sure he screamed like a little girl, yelling in every direction to call for help. When he went to grab his sister and carry her to the car, she swatted his hands aside like he was a nuisance.

"Calm down! Do not freak out. I swear Iian, it's just my water."

"Just your water? Just your water!" He looked around and yelled for one of his chefs. "Have you called Aaron yet?" When he got confirmation, he looked back at his sister. This time she was almost bent over with the pain.

"Screw this," he said, as he walked over and picked her up. "Tell Aaron we're heading to the hospital and to meet us there. We're having this baby now."

Allison and Megan showed up at the hospital less than forty minutes later. By then Lillian Grace Jordan had already been born with the help of the proud daddy.

Aaron stood holding the small bundle on the other side of the glass as everyone gathered around. Todd had the camera and was taking pictures of the wonderful moment. Megan held little Mathew up to the glass, so he could see his small cousin. Iian held Sara who was fast asleep on his shoulder. Allison stood back and smiled at her new family.

Later, when they were able to see Lacey, Iian told everyone the good news.

"A double celebration!" Lacey had exclaimed. She looked wonderful sitting up in her hospital bed. Really, she looked like she had just spent a day at the spa rather than giving birth to a seven-pound baby.

Allison walked over to hug the new mother. Lillian or Lilly, as she was being called by everyone was being held by Megan, who sat on a couch with Matthew and Sara hovering around her.

"I can't believe you're a mother." Allison smiled at her friend. "It seems like just yesterday we were dressing up my Barbie dolls and playing with Play-Doh."

"Don't, you're going to make me cry." Lacey waved a hand in front of her face. "Megan, I love you sister, but if you don't give me my baby, I may have to hurt you," she smiled.

"I think it's time we all left the new family. We'll see everyone tomorrow." Megan handed the small bundle to her sister-in-law. Looking up at her husband, she smiled and silently wished for another child.

By the time Iian and Allison walked in the door of the house, her head felt numb.

"I love your family," she said, later.

"They love you and I love you." She could get used to hearing him say that.

School was officially out. She hadn't been this excited since she was in school herself. The last week of school had dragged on. Every class had seemed like it had been doubled in time.

Now as Iian drove her home, she was actually looking

forward to having a week off before she started teaching at the boys and girls club.

Knowing that the summer classes would be less demanding, she looked forward to spending more time in her studio.

Ric had planned a visit in a few weeks and she wanted to be able to give him the four pieces that she had donated to the Alzheimer Project. She'd spent a lot of time re-making them and felt that they had ended up better than the original ones.

Megan had planned a birthday celebration for Todd over the weekend. They decided to take the yacht out with the family for a fishing trip and had invited them along. The water was still so much a part of Todd's life, that Iian hadn't flinched at the request. Instead, he had agreed without a second thought. His brother's birthday had almost always been celebrated on the water. Even his own birthday had been celebrated this way, at least until his eighteenth.

Still, his brother respected what had happened, so when they did go out, they never traveled too far from the shore.

So, he found himself standing on the deck of the family's larger yacht. Next to him stood the woman that was going to be his wife. He liked saying that over and over in his head. They held hands and watched the shoreline disappear.

It wasn't until an hour later that the shakes were so bad that he had to go below deck. Allison had watched him go, and he knew that it wouldn't be long before she followed him.

When he got below, he closed his eyes and tried his deep breathing exercises. Nothing was helping him. He felt a hand on his shoulder and almost jumped at the light contact.

"Are you alright?" Allison looked into his face and noticed how pale it was.

Walking into his arms, she pulled his face down to hers and lightly ran her lips over his. Distraction was her only thought. As his mouth heated on hers, she started melting into his embrace.

His hands started moving over her hips and when he started to pull her jean skirt up, she tried to back away. "Iian, your family is just upstairs."

"They're busy. I'm sure they know what we're up to. Please, Ally, I need you, I need this."

His hands finished raising her skirt to expose her bright yellow swimsuit underneath. Pulling it down he pushed his fingers inside her and had her gasping and holding onto him. Her fingers dug into his arms, her legs turned to rubber. His kisses deepened and turned to desperate.

With her head back and her eyes closed, he focused on one thing, pleasing her. Soon the rocking of the boat faded and in its place was the sights and smells of Allison. She filled his vision, filled his senses.

He pulled her around and positioned her over the cushion of the large couch that ran down one side of the cabin. Quickly he pulled his swim shorts down and plunged into her slick heat.

Soon, he set his own rhythm, rocking back and forth, causing his own pleasure and hers.

Allison bit her lips on a moan, and when she felt his speed quicken, she knew she would go over the edge with him.

A while later, they joined Todd and Megan up above. Both of them were totally relaxed and Iian showed no more signs of being stressed or nervous. Everyone seemed to enjoy the rest of the weekend on the water.

When they returned home late Sunday evening, they sat on the back patio and ate dinner. The simple turkey sandwiches, which she had whipped up, were delicious. They watched the sunset and talked about their future.

Iian wanted a summer wedding. He claimed he'd waited over twenty years for her and didn't feel like waiting anymore, and she didn't see anything wrong with that. So they spent the rest of the evening making plans and talking about their future.

CHAPTER 18

*H*er first day of teaching art at the Boys and Girls Club was off to a great start. She'd arrived early, thanks to getting her car back from Rusty's last week.

Her multiple weekly visits to her mother were going better. It seemed to her that her mother's mental condition had stabilized at the Hotel. She'd even gained back a little of the weight she'd lost before Allison had arrived home. Her mother still sometimes forgot who she was, but Ally was learning to deal with these times.

Now as she looked over the dozen kids of various ages that were all engrossed in their art projects, she smiled at the thought of her and Iian having children. He really would be a great father.

He'd voiced his concerns about not being able to hear if the baby was crying, but then they had gone online and found a baby monitor for the deaf.

He could carry it around like a pager and it would vibrate like his cell phone. They had spent hours hunched over his laptop looking at other baby devices, toys, and clothes. Even buying a few things for Lilly, Sara, and Matthew. It had been such fun that she could hardly wait for their marriage.

She'd shipped her art to New York where Ric was working with the project for a special auction that would benefit the foundation. She and Iian were going to fly there and attend the special event the following month.

Looking around the large room that housed her art class, she noticed that Tommy and Susie were there today. Both of the children had changed a lot. Tommy no longer drew violent scenes and Susie's drawings were of flowers and other animals. No monsters in sight.

While she enjoyed seeing most of her regular students in the class, and there were a few new faces of older kids. Most of the children attending her classes were at the club for the whole day of summer camp. Only a few were there just for her class, such as the Williams' children.

Brenda their mother, came and picked them up shortly after class was over. Allison could see a slight change in her as well. She'd only seen her a few times since graduation. Gone was the bouncy cheerleader; instead she saw a woman who was frail, thin, and looked like she needed a few pounds and hours of good sleep.

Today, however, Brenda looked a little more like her old self. She had gotten her hair done and it appeared that she was taking better care of her outward appearance. She could tell that some of the woman's confidence was coming back.

Allison remembered when Megan had arrived in town, she had looked and acted a lot like Brenda had. It was hard to imagine a man would treat a woman so terribly.

Then she thought of Iian; he would never lift a finger to anyone. She didn't think there was an ounce of temper in the man. Thinking about it, she couldn't even remember him ever being mad.

Smiling about his good friendly nature, she walked out to her car. She heard a noise to her left and then she noticed Susie crouched down next to a dark car. Dropping her bags, she ran over to the child. Tears were streaming down the little girl's face; her hands and knees were cut as if she'd fallen down.

"Susie, are you alright? Where's your mother?" She looked around. Then she saw the truck. Grabbing the little girl up, she was poised to run, when Kevin interrupted.

"Give me my daughter, you bitch." Turning around slowly, she saw Kevin standing with one hand on Brenda's arm and the other holding his son by the shoulder.

Susie squirmed in her arms and whispered. "I don't want to go with the bad man. Mommy said I wouldn't have to go with him anymore."

"Shh, I won't let you go with him." She comforted the child.

"Susie, come with daddy."

The little girl shook her head no.

Then he screamed, "Get over here!"

"Kevin, you're drunk. Just let us go and we can talk about this," Brenda tried to reason with him.

Allison saw him swaying and realized his eyes were somewhat unfocused, so she started to back up towards her bag and her cell phone.

"Shut up!" He yanked on Brenda's arm and the woman was quiet. "Give me my girl. It's all your fault! If you had learned to mind your own god-damned business, I wouldn't have had to hide away like some outlaw. Do you know that Robert has a warrant out for my arrest? I didn't do a damned thing. This is all your fault," he repeated and turned back towards her.

She watched Tommy squirm under his father's big hands and was relieved to see that, upon focusing his attention on her again, Kevin released the little boy's shoulder. She was even more relieved when the boy took off behind the cars quickly. She silently prayed that he was smart enough to run inside and get help. All she had to do now was stall Kevin from trying to leave or worse.

"Why don't we go inside, and we can…"

"Just shut up! I've never laid a hand on my children. Brenda," he yanked his wife's arm so hard that she cried out. "You tell her. You tell them all, that I've never laid a finger on my kids."

Brenda agreed quickly by nodding her head and Allison watched as tears started to fall down her cheeks.

"Hitting your wife isn't acceptable either." Allison saw the truth.

"I may have slapped her around when I was drunk, but I never raised a hand to my kids. I've lost my wife and kids all because of you. You had to go and ruin everything, you should learn to keep to your own damn business." He was swaying, and she noticed he was trying to pull Brenda towards his truck.

Stall him, Allison thought. Stall him.

Iian was in the middle of an early dinner rush when he received a text from Bob Andrews, the director of the boys and girls club. Iian had talked to Bob about keeping an eye on Allison while she was there for her summer classes. Bob's message said that Kevin had Allison cornered in the parking lot and that he'd called Robert.

Thinking of nothing but Ally and fear for her safety, had him running from the restaurant's back entrance and jumping on his bike, praying that he'd make it in time.

~

"Did you start the fire in my house? Did you hit my mother over the head and leave her for dead?"

He stepped back as if it had been a physical blow.

"I... I just went there to talk to her. To convince her to get you to leave my family alone. The damned woman wasn't making any sense. Then she threatens to call the cops and I grabbed her arm and she fell. I just grabbed her arm. I swear she fell and hit her head on one of those damn candlesticks. I thought she was dead. Then I had to start the fire to cover my tracks."

"Oh, Kevin!" Brenda said beside him. She tried to pull out of his grip, but he tightened it.

"I noticed your car that day in Edgeview. You'd cost me, my family. So, I just pulled out my hunting knife and used it on your tires, so you could pay. You cost me, my family! Then I saw you leaving Walmart. I thought I would just nudge you off the road. Scare you a bit."

He chuckled. "I ended up with a flat tire myself thanks to that crazy driving of yours. That's why I never let Brenda drive my truck. Can't trust a woman behind a wheel."

Allison heard it then, she knew the sound of Iian's

motorcycle anywhere. Keep him talking, she told herself, so he wouldn't hear it.

"I swear I never wanted to hurt your mother. I would never hurt my kids. I just want them back. I miss my boy so much." He turned to look down at where Tommy was, but he'd been long gone. "Tommy!" Kevin shouted. "Get back here boy! We're going to go camping." He tried to make it sound fun. "You, your mom, and your sisters and I are going to take a fun trip," he yelled out to the empty parking lot.

Iian's bike came to a stop just between them. She watched as Iian slowly pulled his leg over the bike and took his helmet off.

"How's it going, Kevin?" Iian asked in a calm voice.

"Get the hell out of my way Iian!" Kevin screamed. "You've always been a thorn in my side. I just want to grab my kids and wife and take a little trip."

He watched as Allison backed up to her car and quickly place the little girl inside. She was standing with her keys in her hand, sheltered the little girl's view from anything that might happen. She looked ready for a fight with her legs spread wide, she had a warrior look about her. She was more beautiful than he'd ever seen her before.

"You aren't going anywhere," Iian said in a calm voice and took a step towards Kevin. "Let Brenda go, and I'll let you off easy." He was calculating how drunk Kevin was. He'd seen him falling down drunk, this was just a small step up from there.

Kevin tried to pull Brenda back towards the truck,

putting Brenda between him and Iian. Iian knew that he couldn't let Kevin get to the truck, he was too drunk to drive. But Kevin stumbled in the process of pulling them towards the vehicle, which gave Iian a perfect opening. In that instant, Iian was on the man. His fist had moved so quickly, Kevin didn't have a chance to defend himself. It had done exactly what Iian hoped it would, Kevin's hands automatically went to his face, releasing Brenda.

Brenda scurried back a few steps out of her husband's reach. Her face was pale, and she looked shocked, her hands went to her mouth as she screamed when Kevin tried to swing at Iian. But Iian's fist smashed into him again, this time taking Kevin to his knees. Just then Iian looked over as Robert's cruiser drove up and parked right behind his bike.

Iian stood over Kevin "I told you I'd let you off easy." Iian hauled Kevin up and waited for Robert to take him off his hands.

"Are you okay?" Robert asked him.

"I'm fine," he looked over and watched Brenda rush to Megan's car and take Susie in her arms. Just then Tommy came running out with Bob, the boy went into his mother's waiting arms as well.

"Is everyone alright?" Robert called over to the group.

"Yes, I think we're fine," Allison said and signed, smiling down at the family. She looked up at Robert and said, "He admitted to everything, running me off the road, slashing my tires, attacking my mother and starting the fire."

"Damn it, Robert! I just wanted to see my kids. There's no harm in that," Kevin was saying as Robert lead him to the car, blood flowed from his nose and lips.

"Kevin, you're under arrest," Robert said and proceeded to give him his rights.

Iian walked over to Allison. "Are you okay?" he signed. He'd been so scared since getting the text message. Fear of losing her, images raced through his mind. He'd never been this scared in his life. He knew that his life would have no meaning without her in it.

"Yes, thank you." She went into his waiting arms. He noticed she was shaking and realized he was shaking as well. Bending his head down, he took her mouth for a kiss that would be etched in his memory for the rest of his life.

EPILOGUE

*J*ian stood on his cliff and looked out over the water. The winter weather was quickly coming. He could sense a large storm brewing and knew it would reach them later that night. Then there was a light tug on his hand and he looked over to his wife of two months.

They had just come back from their honeymoon. Spending a whole month in Paris at Megan and Todd's chateau had been perfect. They'd enjoyed the city, country, food, and sights, but most of all, they'd enjoyed each other.

Allison looked beautiful. Her long blonde hair was flowing in the cold breeze. The salty spray from the water hit them both in the face. His old gray jacket was zipped up to shield her from the crisp wind.

Smiling over at her he said, "A storm's coming."

Allison smiled back at him. Thinking of all the changes that had happened to her over the last year, she was thankful that she'd returned home when she had. "I can't wait for summer again."

"Why is that? It's just ended." He turned and held her other hand and looked into her face.

"Because that's when our baby will be here." She smiled at him.

He blinked a few times. "I'm sorry. Could you repeat that?" He looked dumbfounded.

Pulling her hands free, she signed. "Our baby will be here next summer." She smiled as she was being spun around in circles, listening to her husband laugh with joy.

LASTING PRIDE — PREVIEW

*S*he could feel her muscles screaming. Her arms shook as she pulled herself up to the window and peeked inside. The shaking had nothing to do with the ninety-degree weather or the fact that she'd strained her tiny arms to pull her ninety-five-pound body up five feet. If someone had asked her, she would have denied that they shook because she was scared. She was a Shadow, and Shadows didn't get scared. No matter what! She peeked into the dark window as she moved her tiny body and got a better hold on the narrow ledge. The old place had sat empty for years; now, however, she could see boxes piled up across the dark room and right in the middle of those boxes sat a small safe. *Bingo*.

Billy would be so proud. He might be a little pissed that she hadn't invited the gang along for the job, but he would overlook it for the loot she was sure to bring back. She knew this old place like the back of her hand; after all, she'd lived in the building for over a year. It was the year right after her old man had ended up dead on the sidewalk outside their hotel room.

She cupped her hands and checked the place out, just to make sure it was empty. She could smell the new paint and noticed that the walls were no longer a dingy brown. Someone had painted them a nice glossy white, making them look new, which actually worked in her favor. Now she would be able to see in the dark better. The light from the streets angled in the tall windows and reflected off the high-gloss walls, illuminating the whole room. She wouldn't even need the penlight that was tucked in her pocket.

Reaching into her other pocket, she pulled out the small knife that her old man had lifted for her tenth birthday. She expertly flipped it open and jammed it under the windowsill, searching for the small lock she knew so well. There! The window creaked then slid open silently. Pulling her agile body over the sill, she slowly slid down to the hardwood floor, listening to the whole time and keeping her eyes peeled, just like her old man had taught her.

Hearing and seeing nothing out of sorts, she moved with grace across the floor. Her dirty Keds didn't make a sound on the floorboards. She knew which boards would creek and easily avoided them. Halfway across the room, she heard a siren in the distance, and just for a minute, her heart stopped. She stood motionless, waiting, holding her breath, ready to sprint out the window and run for her life. When the sirens started fading, she released her breath in a soft whoosh.

Moving a little faster, she reached the safe. Perfect! It was an older model and she thought she could easily crack this one in her sleep. Leaning over and placing her ear to the cool metal door, she got to work.

It took her almost five minutes to crack the damn thing. She could blame it on the lack of light, but the truth was that her sweaty hands kept slipping on the cool knob. Finally, when the safe door slid silently open, a huge smile appeared on her face. She was seventeen years old and the best thief in Portland, Oregon. Well, she'd been the best ever since her old man had died of a stroke.

Inside the small safe was a treasure. There was over a thousand in cash, which she quickly rolled up and placed in her pocket. There was a large stack of checks, which she left alone. A small black box sat in the back of the safe. Reaching in, she grabbed the silk case and quickly stashed it in her jacket pocket. This was the best haul since she and her old man had broken into the liquor store. She'd been nine at the time and thought they'd hit the jackpot with three thousand dollars. Not to mention her father had grabbed enough liquor to last him a month.

She pulled out the packet of baby wipes from her pocket and wiped the outside of the safe down like she'd been taught, making sure to go over the handle three times. Then she closed the safe with a small click, spun the dial, stuffed the wipes in her jeans, and let herself out of the old building onto Main Street.

An hour later, she made her way over to the base of the Shadows. They weren't the best-known gang in Portland, but they were her family.

As she crawled through the broken fence, Johnny, tonight's lookout, sat on the ground cross-legged, smoking a cigarette.

"Billy's pissed," he said and flicked the butt across the yard.

It was the simple statement that stopped her. She thought of turning around and playing it cool for a couple of days, but instead, she held her chin up and marched in the back door. This week's base was nothing more than an old bowling alley that had half burned down three months ago. No one drove by, and no one bothered them since the neighborhood had gone down the toilet years ago.

She walked into the small room, which hadn't been burned, at the back of the building. She noticed that Bonnie, her best friend, was sprawled across Billy's lap on an old green couch.

The pair had been together since they were six years old after running away from their foster parents. It had taken several years for the relationship to turn from brotherly and sisterly into what it was today. Rob looked up to them and hoped someday to find something close to what they had.

"Where you been, little girl?" Billy asked without taking his eyes off Bonnie. At the sharpness of his voice, Rob cringed. Bonnie sat up and stretched.

"Just strolling," Rob said, dropping the cash on the table in front of the pair. "Thought you might like to eat out tonight." Rob plopped down and sat cross-legged on the floor, leaning against an old leather chair.

"Where did you get this?" Bonnie asked, as she reached over and started to count the money. Billy looked at Rob and, as much as she knew he didn't want to let it show, Rob could tell he was proud.

"Is this how it's going to be? Are you going off on your own all the damn time, not including your family?

Damn it, Rob!" He pushed Bonnie off his lap and walked over to pull Rob up by her elbows. "We're a family here, and damn it, if you can't respect that, you can use the door. Got it?"

They were nose to nose now and she could smell the beer. Just for a second, she flashed back to a memory. It wasn't Billy digging his fingers into her skin, but her old man, and this time he wouldn't stop at a simple slap or push. This time it would be bad.

She was shaken out of it when Bonnie said, "Billy, leave her alone!" Bonnie sat down with the cash in her hands. "There's over a thousand here."

Billy turned back to Rob. "Where the hell did you get it?"

"No place just fell from the sky, I guess." Rob took a step forward and challenged Billy. "You want to say otherwise?"

For what seemed like a lifetime, the two battled silently with their eyes. Then Billy blinked and smiled. "Fine, little girl, you have your secrets. Let's go get some grub. I'm starved."

The Shadows consisted of fourteen members and the gang was growing bigger every day. The youngest member was eleven and the oldest was Billy at eighteen.

Rob was second in command, not only because of her age but because of her talent. She was the only member who had received a full education. She'd gone to school and, at fifteen, she had gotten her damn GED. It wasn't as if she was a super genius or anything. She just had a really good memory and picked up on every detail. It wasn't her fault things just stuck. Anyway, her old man had been proud. So proud, in fact, that after she'd received her

229

diploma, he'd taken them out and had gotten wasted. Then he'd robbed a local mart and had beaten the crap out of her a few hours later. Rob didn't want to owe anybody anything and even though the Shadows called her family, she knew exactly what they were.

The three of them made their way over to the local Chuck E. Cheese for some cheese pizzas and root beer. As they walked the few blocks, they ran into other members of the gang. Soon there were eight of them walking along the dark road, and Rob had to admit that she felt more comfortable in the large group.

They were half a block away when she heard the low rumble of the car engine. Looking up, she saw the lights before anyone else did. It seemed like a lifetime, but in reality, it had taken less than a minute for her entire world to change.

This is a work of fiction. Names, characters, places, and incidents either are the product of the author's imagination or are used fictitiously, and any resemblance to actual persons, living or dead, business establishments, events or locales is entirely coincidental.

RETURNING PRIDE

DIGITAL ISBN: 978-1-942896-20-3

PRINT ISBN: 9781484949283

Copyeditor: Erica Ellis – inkdeepediting.com

ALSO BY JILL SANDERS

The Pride Series

Finding Pride

Discovering Pride

Returning Pride

Lasting Pride

Serving Pride

Red Hot Christmas

My Sweet Valentine

Return To Me

Rescue Me

The Secret Series

Secret Seduction

Secret Pleasure

Secret Guardian

Secret Passions

Secret Identity

Secret Sauce

The West Series

Loving Lauren

Taming Alex

Holding Haley

Missy's Moment

Breaking Travis

Roping Ryan

Wild Bride

Corey's Catch

Tessa's Turn

The Grayton Series

Last Resort

Someday Beach

Rip Current

In Too Deep

Swept Away

High Tide

Lucky Series

Unlucky In Love

Sweet Resolve

Best of Luck

A Little Luck

Silver Cove Series

Silver Lining

French Kiss

Happy Accident

Hidden Charm

A Silver Cove Christmas

Entangled Series – Paranormal Romance

The Awakening

The Beckoning

The Ascension

Haven, Montana Series

Closer to You

Never Let Go

Holding On

Pride Oregon Series

A Dash of Love

My Kind of Love

Season of Love

Tis the Season

Dare to Love

Where I Belong

Wildflowers Series

Summer Nights

Summer Heat

Stand Alone Books

Twisted Rock

For a complete list of books:

http://JillSanders.com

ABOUT THE AUTHOR

Jill Sanders is a New York Times, USA Today, and international bestselling author of Sweet Contemporary Romance, Romantic Suspense, Western Romance, and Para-normal Romance novels. With over 55 books in eleven series, translations into several different languages, and audio-books there's plenty to choose from. Look for Jill's bestselling stories wherever romance books are sold or visit her at jillsanders.com

Jill comes from a large family with six siblings, including an identical twin. She was raised in the Pacific Northwest and later relocated to Colorado for college and a successful IT career before discovering her talent for writing sweet and sexy page-turners. After Colorado, she decided to move south, living in Texas and now making her home along the Emerald Coast of Florida. You will find that the settings of several of her series are inspired by her time spent living in these areas. She has two sons and off-set the testosterone in her house by adopting three furry little ladies that provide her company while she's locked in her writing cave. She enjoys heading to the beach, hiking, swimming, wine-tasting, and pickleball with her husband, and of course writing. If you have read any of her books, you may also notice that there is a love of food, especially sweets! She has been blamed for a few added pounds by her assistant, editor, and fans... donuts or pie anyone?

facebook.com/JillSandersBooks

twitter.com/JillMSanders

bookbub.com/authors/jill-sanders

CPSIA information can be obtained
at www.ICGtesting.com
Printed in the USA
LVHW021301100921
697438LV00014B/953

9 781942 896210